D1527250

# THE HOUSE OF NORDQUIST

## A NOVEL

## Eugene K. Garber

Transformations Press

Published in Danvers, Massachusetts by Transformations Press.

Mail:    Transformations Press
         85 Constitution Lane 300-C4
         Danvers, MA 01923
Phone:  978-395-1292
Email:   info@transformationspress.org
Website: transformationspress.org


Library of Congress Control Number:  2018936803

Publisher's Cataloging-In-Publication Data

Names: Garber, Eugene K.
Title: The House of Nordquist : a novel / Eugene K. Garber.
Description: Danvers, MA : Transformations Press, [2018] | Series: [The
    Eroica trilogy] ; [3]
Identifiers: ISBN 9781732103801 | ISBN 9781732103818 (ebook)
Subjects: LCSH: Composers--New York (State)--Fiction. | Holocaust
    survivors--New York (State)--Fiction. | Arson--New York
    (State)--Fiction. | Control (Psychology)--Fiction. | Ambition--
    Fiction. | LCGFT: Detective and mystery fiction. | Gothic fiction.
Classification: LCC PS3557.A63 H68 2018 (print) | LCC PS3557.A63
    (ebook) | DDC 813/.54--dc23


Printed in the United States of America.

OTHER BOOKS BY EUGENE K. GARBER

*Metaphysical Tales*
*The Historian*
*Beasts in Their Wisdom*
*Vienna ØØ*
*O Amazonas Escuro*


OTHER TRANSFORMATIONS PRESS BOOKS

*The Art of Balance*
*Paths to Wholeness*
*52 Flower Mandalas*
*52 (more) Flower Mandalas*

*O, might I see hell, and return again,*
*How happy were I then!*

Alice and Paul are sitting at the kitchen table watching the long summer dusk fade. A candle burns inside the chimney of a lamp with a metal base. Outside the window a basket of red begonias flares defiantly against the dying of the day. The needles of the silver spruce are still. In the ash the quarreling of birds has ceased.

Alice looks up from the candle. Where did Eric come from? I don't mean by birth from Deirdre and his crazy father. I mean after being born, or maybe before being born.

Black box.

And where did the music come from? I know it came from Helene's body and went through the machine, but where was it before that?

Black box.

You don't want to talk about this, do you?

Not much.

We have to.

Why?

Black box. Gotcha. Actually I hate black boxes. They're the only thing I hate. I don't hate Eric, because he was crazy. I don't hate the machine, because a machine is just a machine.

If you hate black boxes, we can stop talking about this.

I have an intuition.

About what?

About the fire. That it's going to come up again.

The fire was twenty years ago. What's going to make it come up?

It's in lots of old movies. Unsolved mysteries always come back up. The mad woman in the attic, the bodies walled up in the basement. So we need to talk about the fire.

All right, talk about the fire.

We have to talk about the stuff that came before the fire first. What about the black book? Was the music in it? Can you put music in a book?

I don't know. Eric never showed me what was inside the book. I was just the straight man.

That's what I was to Deirdre. The straight woman. Except there's no such thing as a straight woman, is there? All the straights are men. But what if I was more than Deirdre's straight woman?

Like what?

I don't know. Maybe she needed something I had.

For a while you were Cassandra. She was a straight woman, you could say.

Who was Cassandra?

A prophetess the other characters wouldn't listen to.

What other characters?

The king and queen in the citadel, all the courtiers, the citizens in the chorus.

That's me all right. The king and queen of the House of Nordquist wouldn't listen to me. Actually I didn't care if anybody listened to me except you. But you were totally hung up on Eric. You wanted him to use your body, didn't you?

Yes.

Even though he wouldn't even call you by name.

He didn't call anybody by name.

Maybe when he was by himself he whispered names to the dark powers.

Maybe.

By the end he didn't have a name for anything.

That's right.

You had to say everything for him.

I said what came into my mind.

OK, but he put it there.

Black box.

Right. In the black box of your brain. He had you pegged for a word man from the start. But now you don't say much of anything. You used up all your words with Eric and the Professor. Or are they still up there trying to get out of the black box?

They're still up there.

Me too. I said whatever Deirdre wanted me to. I was the straight woman. But the words are still in my head. It was just a game anyway.

To me you were Cassandra.

Where did Cassandra get what she said, that nobody listened to?

From the future. She was a prophetess.

You didn't have to be a prophetess to figure out that Eric's thing was going to end bad.

I didn't figure it out.

I did. I said so. I didn't even think about it. The words were right there on the tip of my tongue. I let them jump right off like little frogs. Skip the mind. What do you think about that?

Quit gaming me. I'm not Deirdre.

It's not gaming, it's funning. You don't know whether I'm funning you or not. Black box. What's the answer to my question?

What was the question?

What do you think about letting words just jump right off your tongue?

That's probably what you were hoping to do when you tried to learn how to channel.

Maybe. But it didn't work.

Who were you hoping to channel?

I didn't have anybody too particular in mind. Just somebody from the beyond. Julius Caesar, Jesus.

Maybe you should've started a little less ambitiously.

Actually somebody was coming, but I couldn't stand the voltage is the way they put it, so they took me off line in case I might get hurt.

\* \* \*

Please make yourself comfortable, Ms. Albright.

You can call me Alice.

May I stick with Ms. Albright?

Rule of your organization?

Yes, an agency policy. I want to begin by thanking you for giving us the letters between your husband and Professor Tyree. They are proving very useful.

I read them. They weren't useful to me. A lot of words and big ideas. And then that last one from Professor Tyree with the dreams was obviously from a crazy person.

We can talk about that later. You seem uneasy, Ms. Albright.

I'm just looking around. I was in one of these mobile things once before.

What were you there for?

I was giving blood to the Red Cross. I have a rare type, O negative.

Where was this?

Here. I've never left here. They brought a big white box on wheels like this into town. I never gave again.

Why?

It made me dizzy. I had to drink a lot of Coke.

You don't have to worry about that here.

I know. You just want words, not blood, right?

Right.

Do they allow you to go to vampire movies?

It's not a question of allowing. They're not useful.

Maybe going to those vampire movies as a kid made me squeamish about giving blood. Of course it wasn't in the neck but in the arm. Still, I'm glad there wasn't a mirror because my face would've been pasty. Maybe you wouldn't want a mirror here, but it would be nice if you had some posters on the wall.

Over the years we've learned that extraneous images interfere with memory.

The posters in the Red Cross mobile were just medical, like an eye chart with black letters. I couldn't read the bottom line. I don't think it had anything to do with loss of blood.

Probably not.

My husband would say black box, meaning we can't know for sure, or that there isn't anything to know. What's your agency's policy on black boxes?

That whatever is not now known can potentially be known.

What about the thoughts of a dead person at a particular time in the past?

Did you have some deceased in mind?

No. I could think of some, but I didn't have anybody in mind just now. I just thought there might be some things you can't know because they are buried with the dead as they say. I will go to my grave without ever telling is a famous line from old movies.

I see your point. We can only work with known facts. We keep assembling them and putting them together until we have a degree of probability so high that it becomes essentially a certainty.

I get it. Like when I looked at the colorblind charts in the Red Cross mobile I could make out the numbers and shapes with a very high degree of probability, even the number five and the sailboat, which were harder. You know the charts I mean with all the little colored pebbles?

Yes.

My husband could've seen them in a snap.

Does he have special visual powers?

More like he has the ability to go right into something. It's hard to explain.

It sounds like a case of intense concentration.

He would erase everything around the number 5 pebbles until there was nothing else left in the universe. If you were standing there you would get erased with everything else.

That's extraordinary, Ms. Albright.

Yes, but here's something I've been wondering about. Why would the colorblind charts have numbers instead of letters?

The system was invented by a Japanese doctor. He didn't want to use ideograms, probably because Westerners couldn't identify them.

Interesting. I'll bet my husband was into ideograms, but we never talked about it.

We can ask him when we find him.

I don't think you're going to find him. And even if you do, I doubt he'll tell you anything you don't already know about the fire.

* * *

It is dark. In the kitchen window the only thing that can be seen is the reflection of the candle on the table. Alice is speaking.

Deirdre didn't want my body, even to paint it, though one time she said she might paint my hair. Eric didn't want your body. Couple of body type losers. But you know what?

What?

I think what I just said was not true. I think maybe Deirdre did want my body for something, but right now I don't know what. I'm thinking about it.

Let me know when you figure it out.

I started to ask if you thought Deirdre was sucking the colors from Helene's body the way Eric was sucking the sound, but I don't think Helene had any colors left when she got to the House of Nordquist. Do you?

I don't know.

There was her naked body lying on that stone right under your eyes day after day, and you don't know if it had any colors. You know what? I believe you.

Thanks.

It was before you got good at erasing everything else around something. Which explains why when Deirdre brought Eric the black book of paintings you didn't see that either.

I saw the book, but I couldn't see inside it.

Right. In the old movies when the camera doesn't want you to see some awful scene it just shows somebody's eyes, which get wide like Peter Lorre's. I know why you couldn't see the paintings.

Why?

You let yourself get sucked into the scene. You can't see the scene if you're inside it.

Good point.

You remember the junk Deirdre painted before she started on the black book?

Yes.

Water colors of the same landscape, the same hills and clouds and trees, the same blue river, the same smiling sun, no boats, no birds, no people, not even stick figures.

I remember.

Then Eric told her to paint music in the black book. Some time I'm going to figure out what it looked like.

I look forward to that.

OK, but right now we have to talk about Eric. Eric had powers. You wished he used his powers on you instead of Helene.

And you wished Deirdre would paint you in the black book.

Right. It would've been my once in a lifetime as a model. Eric and Deirdre were once in a lifetime people. Like they said about the old movie stars. They had IT, capital IT. What was IT?

Magnetism, mesmerizing auras, pulsations.

Where did Eric get IT?

Black box.

Maybe he got IT from sailing to the Arctic with his insane father. Maybe they sailed all the way north until they got to the edge and looked over, and right there was IT. The old man couldn't stand the voltage and cracked up, but Eric brought IT back. What do you think?

I think you're close. The old man wanted to find absolute zero. And maybe he did, but Eric left him there and came back. It's an old story, sailing off to get some great prize.

Like what?

Helen of Troy, the Golden Fleece, the New World.

The candle on the table flares momentarily, a defect of wick or wax.

I'm not going to look out the window anymore. It's one of your black boxes.

The window's not a black box. You can see a little bit of the tree and flowers outside. You can see our faces on the glass.

It's a black box.

* * *

To tell you the truth I get tired of remembering. It was hardly a month ago my husband and I sat in the kitchen after supper trying to get it all straight.

Just what were you trying to get straight?

The fire and everything that led up to it.

Why were you trying to get it straight?

I told my husband that unsolved mysteries always come back. That's why you're here, isn't it? Asking all these questions. But I can tell you that trying to get something like the fire straight is hopeless.

That's why I'm here all right, but it's not hopeless.

I thought at first you were with a TV company. Unsolved Mysteries or Open Case.

We're not interested in crime, Ms. Albright. Just the facts.

Just the facts. I remember that saying. It was in a radio show about a detective. I think his name was Jack. He kept knocking on doors and encountering hysterical women and having to tell them that he just wanted the facts. But I'm wondering why you waited twenty years to get the facts.

We're a relatively new agency, Ms. Albright, so we have a backlog. Soon we'll be on the scene right after every event.

What about all the lost facts from old scenes?

Facts never get lost permanently. They are always recoverable. In this instance you and your husband are key.

I don't think you're going to find my husband, but if you do, he'll tell you that the story of the fire is inside a black box.

That's where we always start, Ms. Albright, with a black box. But why do you think we won't find your husband?

Because I couldn't find him, even when he was sitting right across the table from me. He has the disappearing act down pat.

We often have to start with things that have disappeared.

You're probably thinking of a dark alley or basement hideout or a mustache and dyed hair. I'm talking about really disappearing, like the invisible man in the movies.

There's never been a case of an invisible man, Ms. Albright.

I told you he could go right into a colorblind chart or any other place he wanted to. You couldn't see him. He wouldn't see you. You'd be erased.

You didn't get erased when you talked with him about the fire.

No, but I was only a half face in candlelight or a ghost in the window.

What place do you think your husband has gone into now?

Any place where Eric might be.

We don't know that Eric is alive.

I'm sorry, but you'll have to tell me again about the remains.

We have remains for three individuals, but we can determine DNA from only two. The two identifiable sets don't match. That means that any one of the four persons in the house could have escaped.

Maybe nobody escaped.

Evidence makes that highly unlikely.

You said remains. You mean ashes and pieces of bones?

No, you can't get DNA from those.

What did you get it from?

I'm not at liberty to tell you, but we made a very fortunate find that the earlier investigators missed.

Now you've got me going. I'm imagining some kind of buried urn with organs in it. I guess I watched too many horror movies.

It was nothing like that.

What about a DNA match for me?

There isn't any. We have no evidence that the son you reported lost in the fire was in fact there.

He was there. I saw him just before the roof timbers fell. He went from red to pure white. There wouldn't have been any remains.

It was a very intense fire, but we believe we have remains from anybody who was lost in it.

Really? You've been up on that hill. You know how the wind blows everything away.

It's not absolutely impossible that some remains have been lost, but it's highly improbable. We don't use the highly improbable to form plausible hypotheses.

OK, but if you have DNA samples, can't you find matches from samples from where the deceased were before the fire?

Unfortunately not. We could find no samples of Eric's or his mother's outside the house. As for Helene, none were saved from her time at the immigration center, and all of her family that we know of were lost in the war.

What about Professor Tyree?

We got some old samples from the college, but they were badly degraded. We hypothesize at this point that it is very likely the Professor died in the fire.

Hypothesize is interesting. You could hypothesize just about anything. You could hypothesize that with the right equipment you could suck music from a body and change the world. What would you think of that hypothesis?

We would classify that as fantastical.

So would I, but my husband is now searching for the very person that hypothesized that.

What do you think your husband believes Eric is doing?

I think he believes Eric is somewhere with the black book, because if Deirdre painted the whole symphony in it, then Eric didn't need Helene's body anymore. He didn't need any of us anymore. In fact it's a miracle I'm here. If the wind had been blowing the other way, the cinders would have landed on the roof of our house and we would've burned up in our sleep. Anyway, if I were you I wouldn't send men out to find my husband.

You think it's futile.

Or worse.


                              * * *


*Dear Professor John,*

*Thanks for giving me permission to address you as John. But you have always been my teacher, so I'll stick with Professor John.*

*I've been remembering our session on origins. You'll see why. You chose Meachem for your Socratic Other. How the two of you loved to joust. You posed the question. How can we find the origin of this thing called Meachem? The moment before inception? Outmuscling all those others contenders? We all snuffled knowingly, calling up our scraps of biology.*

*Nay, sir! declared Meachem. The true origin cannot admit of randomness.*

*Where then? you asked. In connubial bliss, or even further back in that first meeting that led to the wedlock of progenitors?*

*Nay, sir. You will subject the origin of Meachem to infinite regress and thus forfeit his luminous presence among us.*

*Well spoken. Then let us go the other way, to a moment shortly after birth when the intransigence of a rattle caused Meachem to form his self as a thing of fierce will and perseverance. Can you subscribe to that?*

*Only fractionally, sir, for there must have been many further trials that formed said Meachem as the brilliant oppositional polemicist we observe today.*

*Huzzahs and cheers from us groundlings.*

*Again, well spoken. Thank you, Meachem, for lending us your self for this investigation. We conclude that the concept of the origin is ultimately useless, as is the presumption of foreseeing futurity. The great epicists—Homer, Virgil, Milton—understood that the story always begins in medias res. From that point we shuttle back and forth until memory and prophecy fail us. What finer fate, then, than to be always a thing ultimately unknown and unknowable. Meachem, astrum vagabundum, our wandering star. If only we could grasp him, we would wear him in our heart of hearts.*

*None of us will ever forget it, Professor John. And now the application to the present. You asked me about my first meeting with Eric. It wasn't exactly a meeting but rather a sighting. And if there could be origins, this would certainly have been one. I'll try to render it for you.*

*It was back in early June. I was down by the beach, alone. I had just moved into my father's cottage. He had, as you recall, died during my senior year. I had finished the necessary fix-its. So I took a*

morning off and walked down to the beach. It's formed by an inshore
curl of the river. The water is usually slow and clear, but this day
it was sullied by an army of small feet. Children howling gleefully,
having miraculously escaped the clutches of an icy demon lurking on
the sandy bottom, dashing back up the beach to mothers with warm
towels.

Suddenly there was a flaring of red and white, a tall young
man running swiftly across the sand, hair a torch swept back by the
wind of his running. As he passed close by me, I saw that his flesh,
though pale, was a casing of taut musculature lustrous in the morning light. A moment later this swift courser plunged into the cold
water, disappeared, surfaced, arched, dove again, rose, like a flaring
of unquenched fire.

A woman in a gray caftan with a cincture of white cord awaited
his return. She held up a purple towel that wimpled in the breeze.
He took it and wrapped himself in it, but I could not see that they
touched or spoke to each other.

That's Eric from the House of Nordquist and his mama. This
from a disfigured child, the left side of her face higher than the right.

The House of Nordquist? I said.

Up on the hill. Don't you see it?

I looked up. High on the hill sat a huge house with much glass,
the north wall sharp-edged like the cutwater of a ship. How had I
failed to take in such a strange and imposing thing?

You see it?

Yes.

The girl made a gleeful yelp. I thought you went blind looking
at Eric. It's a ship. See? The old man sailed it. You could hear him
hollering.

Why was he hollering?

Because the ship was in ice. It could sink. That's what they said.
But he's dead now. The child made a queer yodeling and ran off.

I continued to look at the house. Huge sheets of glass formed the
north wall, small round windows elsewhere, steeply pitched roof, a
single door within a tall archway.

Then the red flare again, the white flesh draped in purple followed by a swatch of gray, swimmer and mother ascending the hill.

*The tasseled hood of the caftan failed to hold her hair, which tumbled down her back like a dark shadow.*

*Just then a slice of wind warped the air and the pair disappeared.*

*So, Professor John, not the origin. We have ruled that out. Just a sighting. But of what? Archetype? Avatar? I leave the question with you. I could not put it in better hands.*

*As ever,*
*Paul*

*P.S. I should have said this, that my memory of the flying figure is not continuous. It is composed of separate images rapidly changed like those old timey shutter-box shows, as if inviting me to stop the stuttering illusion of unbroken motion and see the thing as it is.*

* * *

I'm returning the original of the letters between your husband and Professor Tyree. I repeat, the agency extends its gratitude to you for letting us copy them.

Thanks, but I figured you could demand anything you wanted.

We avoid demands, Ms. Albright. Unwilling sources are rarely useful.

To tell you the truth, I'd forgotten all about the letters. I found them rooting around in my husband's desk looking for clues about where he's gone.

Did you find any clues?

No.

What we find striking about the letters is that each writer almost seems to know what the other one is thinking.

They were very close in those days.

Unfortunately it's not possible to determine for sure that we have all of their letters.

I didn't hold any back. My husband said Deirdre gave him the ones he wrote to Professor Tyree the day before the fire, but he didn't remember right. My younger son saved them from the fire. You could still smell how the paper was scorched. Then he went back into the burning house. I couldn't stop him.

Why did he go back in?

He must've thought there was something else to save.

Such as?

A tape of Eric's symphony maybe. Or the black book.

Which you say contained paintings of Eric's symphony. Do you mean graphic notation?

I don't know what that is.

Images of sounds instead of notes on bars.

Something like that.

You were twenty-three at the time of the fire. How old was this son?

I know what you're going to say. You have no remains that match my DNA. And I'm going to say the same thing. The wind has been blowing across the hill for twenty years since the fire.

Do you think it would be possible for someone to escape from the rear of the house?

There wasn't any rear of the house. That part was all ship. You had to go out through the front door. And there was supposed to be a big pit by the door, but it was imaginary.

Who imagined it?

My husband. He was the only one. If anybody else could have imagine it, it would have been the Professor but even he couldn't.

Could you imagine it?

I could've imagined it, but I didn't need to. My husband already had.

Our records show that at one time you studied to be a psychic.

I did. A woman trainer set up in town. I thought I would give it a try. I didn't have a lot to do anymore. The boys were grown up and gone.

How did it go?

I was supposed to learn how to channel. I turned out to be a flop.

What happened?

I got through to a party from the beyond one time, but I couldn't handle the voltage, as they say.

Whom did you get through to?

My younger son. But I couldn't handle it. It was like electric worms in my ear. I think he may have had the book in his hand, but the room was pitch black.

So you didn't actually see the book.

More like heard it. Music, not words, which is no surprise.

Why do you say that?

Because Eric hated words.

Did you ever try to talk to Eric?

I practically never got near Eric, but if I had he wouldn't have talked to me. At first he talked to my husband a little. He would come back from the House of Nordquist with Eric's words sticking in him like little darts.

Interesting. And then what happened?

Eric stopped talking. Paul had to speak for Eric. He had to say whatever Eric put in his mind.

Did he repeat any of it to you?

Not really. One thing Eric said was raven. Not the bird. But even that wasn't a word.

Yes, that's in the letters. We'll come back to that.

I can't come back to much more today. I know you're just doing your job but it's like fingernails rooting around in my brain.

I understand, but one last thing. Just a minute ago you referred to your boys. You have another son besides the one lost in the fire?

Yes, the older. He's a wanderer. He sends me postcards from exotic places, the pyramids, the Colossus at Rhodes, the hanging gardens of Babylon.

We haven't found any postcards.

After a while I stopped saving them.

Why?

He was always in danger. It scared me.

What kind of danger?

Danger from various savage people. Egyptians, Persians, Phoenicians, Arabs, Aztecs.

Does he ever write you letters?

No. Letters were out of fashion by the time he grew up.

Your sons must've been fairly old when you adopted them.

I considered adoption, but I preferred to have my own sons. Blood line and all that. I'm a little ashamed, knowing how many children need parents.

Did you think about the possibility of not having any children at all?

I know a woman down in the town who wouldn't have any children because she didn't want to bring a child into this world as it is now. I could've told her that that kind of thinking could lead to somebody trying to change the world.

Like Eric.

Yes, your improbable hypothesis.

So you decided to have children.

It's the worst thing that can happen to a woman, being barren. In the Bible, in movies, even if you're beautiful like Elizabeth Taylor. If a husband has a barren wife he'll take his seed somewhere else. Not my husband. He never acknowledged my sons. That's all right. I had their company. My husband was off to himself reading or walking down by the beach in all weathers. So it was good to have them with me, even if one was lost in a fire and the other one went away. They've always been near, mind over matter.

What did your husband read?

I was afraid you would ask that. He didn't actually read in the ordinary way. I would look in on him in his study sometimes. He would have an open book and be looking hard right down into it, but he never turned the page. He must've found some sentence that contained everything he needed. Or maybe he just needed one letter, like an O, and he would get inside it.

Strange.

Yes.

Back to the letters. Would you be willing to go over the letters and note any observations that come to you?

I read the letters after my husband left. I don't want to read them again. I don't understand much of what's in them. There's a big gap between my husband and me in education. What kept us together after that first chemistry, as they call it, was memories. Who else could share memories like ours? Most people wouldn't even believe them. I don't think you do.

* * *

Thin rain is drifting down from a gray sky. The streaked window reflects, like an old mirror, two faces delicately stigmatized as if by failures in the silvering.

I'm remembering Deirdre. Always that gray robe. What do you call it?

A caftan.

Caftan. Like something a nun would have to wear. Very coarse like you were being scratched all the time for something you did wrong.

Yes, but the hood that hung down in the back had a gold tassel.

The gold tassel didn't fit in. Nothing in this story fits in. I used to wonder if she had legs. I never saw any. When she moved, it was more like rolling than walking. You remember?

Yes, as if she were on trundles.

Maybe she didn't have legs.

Right. Prostheses with wheels.

Quit being a smartass. What do you really remember about Deirdre?

I never understood her.

I didn't say understood. I said remember.

To me she was more of a Poltergeist than she was Eric's mother. What's that?

A ghost. Usually of a particular house.

If I was a ghost I wouldn't have picked the House of Nordquist.

I'm not sure Poltergeists get to pick the house.

Nobody in this story got to pick anything except Eric. He picked everything and everybody. Anyway, is that all you remember about Deirdre?

She was extensible.

Meaning?

Meaning that no matter where you were in the house she was there.

How did she do it?

She liquefied herself.

I thought you were going to say she turned herself into fog.

Better. Fog.

It's too bad she never gave you a name like she gave me, Alicia. It would've been something highfaluting. Like Paulus. I bet there's some famous person in history named Paulus.

Not that I know of.

How about Alicia? Any famous Alicia?

There was a bad hurricane named Alicia back when hurricanes were all women.

Very funny. Alicia. That's what she called me from day one. Which was OK with me. I didn't mind playing the game, but now I'm wondering if there was more to it.

Like what?

I don't know, but sometimes if I tripped up and called myself Alice she would get mad because everything in the house had to be a certain way to make it work.

I don't think it would've worked if I'd been Paulus.

No, because you were down in Eric's studio being No-Name. But I don't want to talk about Eric. I want to talk about Deirdre.

Go ahead.

Her voice was like the way she walked, remember? It didn't have any steps to it. It didn't go up or down. Come with me, dear Alicia, the voice said. And the gray caftan floated off with the body inside, if there was a body. Come with me, dear Alicia. And Alicia would tag along because she wanted to know what was going on. Did Alice ever wonder what a person without a body might want from a person that had one? No.

You were getting into your role. It's called method acting.

Like type casting in the movies, right? I was Alicia. You were No-Name. What did it feel like getting into the role of No-Name?

Like being a tabula rasa.

What's that?

An erased tablet.

So he wrote all over you—the words he never said, the pictures Deirdre painted for him, the sounds he got out of Helene's body. Pretty soon you wouldn't have had any room to write yourself. Lucky the fire came. But come to think of it, you had Professor Tyree writing on you too. What was that name he gave you?

Childe Paul.

Why? Because he thought you hadn't grown up?

It's doesn't mean a child. It's spelled with an **e** at the end. It means a young nobleman.

Well, which one did you like best? No-Name or Childe Paul since there wasn't any actual Paul left?

Neither one fit.

Nothing in this story fits. Doesn't matter. You got into your roles because you loved the Professor and Eric.

I wouldn't have put it exactly that way.

I don't mean in love. A lopsided dwarf and a mute maniac. But you were all for them body and soul. It's a torch song in an old movie.

I've heard it.

You never had an inkling of where it was all going?

Maybe. But I had to see it through to the end.

OK, like I was with Deirdre, but it was different because I didn't love her. I just wanted to know what was going on. Funny, isn't it? We were supposed to be the ones that were close, but you were with Eric and I was with Deirdre. And then Helene came. What was she close to, just that stone like some kind of graveyard angel?

She didn't want to be close to anything.

What did she want?

She wanted to give everything up.

\* \* \*

You said you and your husband didn't agree about what happened at the House of Nordquist.

That's right. He went along with the story that it was an accident.

But you don't think so.

No.

Who do you think started the fire?

Some fire demon.

With all due respect, Ms. Albright, that's not helpful.

Demon is a metaphor. Does the agency allow metaphors?

We prefer not to deal in metaphors. But all right, who do you think the demon was?

How about Alice? She had good reasons.

What would they have been?

To get her boyfriend Paul free of Eric. To get rid of Professor Tyree. To get away from Alicia. Burn it all up.

But would Alice want to burn up Deirdre?

Deirdre was not an innocent bystander.

We'll come back to that. But what about Helene?

Helene was already dead for all practical purposes.

* * *

*Dear Childe Paul,*

*If I am to be Professor John, then you must have a noble name. Childe Paul. Childe Paul to the dark tower rode.*

*All hail, Childe Paul. So young and already master of a golden epistolary style. Meanwhile, I go on in my lumpish way, trusting memory, which we know is dangerous. I believe nevertheless I can call up the essence of our first full discussion of Eric Nordquist, which came during a walk we took in the gallery of the famed cloister of Justin and James College for Men. Vaulted, trefoil archways. Not the beach and coil of the cool river in your last letter, but a slow rain of big bellied drops that sounded a lento of droll plops among the leaves of the maples. And not a lean courser with flaring red hair but a gnomish creature, glasses so thick and irregular that the eyes behind them seemed to pulse, like one of those creatures that propels itself by ingesting and disgorging sea water.*

*Back and forth in the gallery, you and John Tyree, Professor of Liberal Studies, notorious man of words. Under the unvarying black beret were, according to student mythology, atrocious lumps and scars, stigmata of a divinely ordained cudgeling that had all but destroyed the eyes, dented the forehead, and bent the little monster forward so that he seemed always poised to plunge into a space already populous with his own words.*

*Who do they say I am? I asked you.*

*Tactfully you declined to answer.*

*Nemo they call me. They have emptied their word cabinets to stuff an effigy, but do not know who I am. Fat, dwarfish, fleshy, tortuous, larded. Lexicon of dunces. But you, Childe Paul, know that protruding forehead and twisted face do not a Quasimodo make. Who do you say I am?*

*You said, you're the only one who would believe me if I told you I have a friend who's going to change the world. Perhaps you thought I would find that ludicrous, but I said, of course you have a friend who's going to change the world. Even here in our own little pastoral collegium grazes a small herd of Weltumformers.*

*But this one is different.*

*In what way?*

*He's dead serious.*

*Where's he to be found?*

*On top of a hill in a house built to look like a ship. He's dead serious.*

*Ah, so this is the courser of fiery red you described earlier. Well, there are always a few e pluribus who truly imagine they are scaling the outworks of Godhead. They might even be tragic, if there were such a thing as tragedy anymore. I probably didn't say it just that way. But I remember vividly executing a deliberate quarter turn. Enter the chorus. Strophe. O King, the streets of the city reek of death.*

*I don't think this is an Oedipal crime story, you said.*

*Every story is a crime story, starting with the Fall. The forbidden tree was planted in the garden by a god that was weary of a world without a shadow of turning.*

*I don't remember that you replied to that. The idea of a world-changer atop a hill in a ship warmed my imagination. Well, you must warn your nautical world-changer that the sagas of the great seafarers have all been swallowed down the gullet of modernism. Stories of huge seas sweeping the deck, masts felled like axed timbers, louring headlands with teeth like tigers, clashing rocks, miraculous landfalls. All gone. Wide and waste the sea. Wagner discovered the horrible truth over a half century before we could understand him. The sea is inane. But never mind. Tell me the story of your world-changer.*

*It begins with the story of his father, who designed the house. He sailed the ship into the Arctic and went mad. I'm not sure exactly what legacy he left his son.*

*That will become clear. For now, tell me how the son will change the world.*

*With a musical composition.*

*A single musical composition?*

*Yes.*

*A single magnum opus. This has potential. What's your world-changer's name?*

*Eric.*

*Norse and kingly.*

*There we ended, at least as I remember. And now you are a frequenter of the House of Nordquist. Write me often, Childe Paul. This story fascinates me. But I worry about your place in it. I remember what you wrote about the way in which your memory of Eric on the beach tends to break apart into a series of stuttering images. Tares planted by the Devil, Professor Aptheker, our resident Lutheran, would call them, capable in their aggregate of hiding from you the true grain.*

*Fondly,*
*Professor John*

* * *

You didn't approve of Eric?

To put it mildly.

Why?

He sucked everybody dry.

What do you mean by that?

I mean until there was no more milk in us. It would happen to me with my older one. I ran out of milk, but that was different.

We can come back to your sons. Let's go on with your metaphor. Did Eric suck his mother dry?

That's the hardest question you've asked so far. I would say yes, he did. He made her stop painting watercolors and start painting his music in the book. He made her go get Helene for him. You could say he sucked up her self.

Interesting, this idea of painting music in the book.

Yes. But we'll never know for sure. A lost fact.

We have reason to believe the book was not destroyed in the fire.

Really? What reason?

It has to do with bindings and certain fiber traces that could be detected after even a very hot fire.

Traces? There were lots of missing traces in the House of Nordquist.

Such as?

The body of the old man. Before Eric quit talking, he told Paul the old man sank through the ice to the bottom of the sea where the fish ate him. But I wonder what they really did with the body.

We know very little about the father. His remains were not discovered. He was not in our database.

Your database? What's in that?

The facts of all cases.

Just facts? No hypotheses?

The hypotheses are recorded in a different sector. It's the facts that enable us to perceive patterns from which to form hypotheses.

Like the dots in a child's picture book, I'll bet. It's on all the newscasts. The dots were there, but nobody connected them. If you connect them, I'd like to see the picture. Was Eric in your database?

Yes.

And Deirdre?

Yes.

Helene?

No.

That's because Deirdre went to the island and got her before they could write down the information about her.

Or they failed to kept their records properly.

You said the facts never get lost permanently.

That's right.

Not even in a fire?

Not even in a fire.

I have a confession to make. I haven't been sticking to the facts. I've been giving you opinions and feelings, like the batty woman on the other side of the door in the movies, even after the detective shows her his badge.

You have no confession to make, Ms. Albright. Opinions and feelings are facts. They fall into a special category we call expressive. We value them because sometimes the only way to get to certain objective particulars is to penetrate a feeling and transform its non-rational elements into a working facticity.

That's interesting. So I can go on telling the story without worrying about sorting out facts and feeling?

Do whatever makes it easy for you.

Well then I'll say something about the old man, who was probably one of the most nonfactual things in the story.

Please do.

I told you, he died in the Arctic and they committed him to the deep. That was the story Paul and Eric played out one afternoon. Only it wasn't a story for Paul. It was real.

It sounds like he had a very vivid imagination.

It wasn't just imagination. I was down in the weeds pouting because Eric wouldn't let me come up to the glass tower and be part of the story. But I could hear Paul hollering that the ship was breaking apart. He was really there, near absolute zero, he told me later. And then everything got totally quiet, frozen solid. What is absolute zero anyway?

A condition of no molecular activity. Some say at that point everything turns to dust and falls apart, but that's probably a metaphor.

My husband wrote poems when he was a student and invented lots of metaphors. Otherwise I wouldn't know about absolute zero and fire demons and things like that.

Right. What else do you know about the father?

Nothing. Deirdre never talked about him. Sometimes I imagined his body was hidden down in the basement, still frozen from the Arctic until the fire thawed him out and he got away.

You have a fine imagination, Ms. Albright.

Is anything I imagine a fact?

That you imagined Gunnar Nordquist was thawed by the fire and ran away is a fact, but we would not pursue it, because it's never likely to be substantiated.

What's not a fact?

Something that has not been introduced into anybody's perception. In other words, a null.

\* \* \*

*Dear Professor John,*

*You wrote that you wanted me to keep you posted. I will, but let me know when you've had enough of the House of Nordquist.*

*Yesterday Eric took me up to the north tower. It really does look like the conning tower of a ship. Its walls (I should say bulkheads) are constructed entirely of steel struts and cross members that hold in place huge sheets of glass. Alice was not allowed to come. From the tower I looked down at her. She was standing in a thicket of weeds topped with heavy seed heads. The wind was whipping them back and forth, stripping away husks, sowing the wild scrabble of the hill.*

Alice's hair, caring nothing for the direction of the wind, tumbled willfully this way and that. To me her hair always seems live. It's not pretty, a run-of-the-mill light brown and always disheveled, but live, and with a fragrance so rich I sometimes imagine I can actually see its aura, especially in the early light that catches briefly the hidden emanations of earth.

From the tower I waved to her. She tilted her face upward but didn't wave back. I have stopped to describe her because even then I knew that I was in the wrong place, that I should have been with her. Why wasn't I? That is the burden of this story.

I looked around the tower. From our reading of Conrad I recognized most of the objects—captain's swivel chair mounted on gimbals, compass mounted on binnacles, wheel, charts, a long glass. Eric stood looking out over the woods that rise in terraced steps toward a sharp escarpment etched against the western horizon.

I waited patiently without speaking, having learned that with Eric one has to endure long silences. So thorough is his distaste for words that one's own words begin to coagulate like a sickening cud in one's throat. After a long contemplation of the landscape he finally turned from the window and with a wave of his hand said, you know where you are? Maybe you thought I was going to say he spoke in a voice as raspy as a rusty hinge. Not so. His voice is perfectly clear and crisp but totally disdainful of itself.

Not exactly I said in answer to his question.

Latitude sixty-six degrees twenty-eight minutes, longitude two degrees twenty-three minutes.

Where are we in the story?

It's not a story. It's a geometry. It's what happens when you wrap the earth in lines. You go to the bottom of the sea, like my father. But if you want a story, tell it.

OK. We're locked in ice. Winter has overtaken us. We're all doomed.

Go on.

Some have made crude sleds from the ship's timbers and gone south. They will never be heard of again.

Eric took me roughly by the arm and led me to the captain's chair and sat me down in it. The leather was hard and cracked. I redirected my gaze from the western escarpment to the irregular cresting of the Catskills in the north.

I continued the story. *The ice is tightening its grip on the ship. She shudders beneath us. The gimbals of the Captain's Chair have frozen stiff. The ice floes bare their teeth like angry bears. The barren moon is frozen in a starless sky. Our voices are thinned by the arctic air. Unceasing winds bow the mainmast and mizzenmast and swell the sails until they belly in taut labor, but the ship cannot move.*

Go on.

*The shrouds and stays, sheathed in ice, sag dangerously. The sails, heavy with ice, are tearing away from the hauls. The masts and spars are turning into giant stalagmites. Razor sharp floes are sheering the strakes off the hull. The cross-members are buckling. The deck is heaving and splintering, the cutwater cracking. We're approaching absolute zero.*

Go on.

I couldn't go on, Professor John. I told Eric he would have to finish the story. He remained silent. We went below. Now here is an enigma. I didn't make up the story. I may have embellished it, but I was inside of it. How does one get inside a story he has never heard before?

Your puzzled student,
Paul

* * *

Did you welcome Professor Tyree's coming?

No.

Why?

Well, for one thing he was ugly as sin. Still, maybe I should've wanted him to come.

Why?

I was losing Paul to Eric. Maybe the Professor could get between them. But it didn't work out that way. I never saw him again after he came by the house. Paul never saw him at all that time. The fire came. Later I read that last letter he wrote to Paul about the dreams, the one he gave to Deirdre to deliver instead of mailing it. Maybe he wrote it on the train. The hand was wiggly. Once I read it I knew he couldn't have done anything to help. And then he burned up in the fire you say.

That's what the fractional sample of DNA points to.

Dreams are facts but not their content, right?

You are a quick study, Ms. Albright.

Thanks. If he burned up in the fire, that would still leave any one of three that got away. I'm not saying anything about my son.

That's the working hypothesis.

OK, here's another fact, expressive you call it, I believe. I don't trust anything the Professor wrote in any of his letters.

Why?

Because they're really love letters, and you can't trust love letters. In the movies the smitten woman opens the letters with trembling hands and drops a tear by mistake right on the word love and smears it.

What were your observations of the Professor when he came by the cottage?

If you mean did he look like a lover, I have to laugh. He was very polite in an old-timey way. I thought he might even tip that little black thing he had on his head.

What did he say?

He made a speech about my husband's brilliance and how glad he was to see me because he knew I was the right companion for my husband. Companion, not sweetheart or anything like that.

But you didn't trust him?

No.

Why?

It's hard to trust somebody you can't stand to look at.

He was that ugly?

Yes, not your ordinary ugly but like King Kong or some monster from an old movie had grabbed him and twisted him in different directions. You figured his words were bound to be twisted too.

Oddly there's no photograph of him in the college archives.

They wouldn't want one. But after the fire I had a reason to think of him differently.

How?

I thought if he got caught in the fire, he wouldn't have any idea how to get away because the flames would come at him in every direction in those thick glasses he wore. His eyes on the other side were so big you could only see parts of them at a time. It made me dizzy thinking of a fire through those glasses. It made me want to pity him.

I can understand that.

Here's another weird fact. When I was trying to learn how to channel, I figured I'd get in touch with the Professor and ask him what Eric's symphony sounded like.

What makes you think he heard the symphony?

Just an intuition. I think it tipped him over. I think he cracked up. It's too bad I never learned how to channel. I know you would have to say that things learned from channeling aren't factual. But our trainer told us that the great thing about channeling was that Spirits on the other side were compelled to tell the truth, whether they wanted to or not.

What do you think the Professor's spirit would've said?

I don't know. But he wouldn't have said the symphony was just Helene's body gurgling and groaning in the machine. It was something bigger than that.

You think it might've been the Professor who started the fire?

If words are flint.

That's clever, Ms. Albright.

Thanks. But talking about the symphony makes me think of Helene. You said she wasn't in your database. Can't you put dead people in your database?

Yes. She's in it now. An unregistered immigrant from Germany.

I thought she wasn't in the records on the island.

Just a scrap, first name and origin.

Maybe she had reasons not to give her last name. But anyway you can put in your database now the story of how she lay wired up on a stone for days on end, until she was just a skeleton.

Yes, and there will be more. The database is never complete.

* * *

*Dear Childe Paul,*

*A propos your last. Don't be alarmed that you told a story you've never heard. Your imagination assembled it out of the details around you. Plato would say that you simply remembered it, that it was always there, one of the most memorable archetypes, the tragic voyage.*

*Mnemosyne. She stretches me on the rack of contrariety, the pleasure of remembering you and the pain of not having you here beside me. I choose to remember. I meet you after lunch one day. Persephone has arisen from the underworld. Spring. I say, shall we take a post-prandial perambulation along the littoral? Professorial pedantry.*

*Always considerate, you let your Professor set the pace down to the river walk, his stumpy mismatched legs barely able to negotiate the moderate decline of the embankment. He says, when Nature makes a monster, it's not without purpose. I could be of service to your friend Eric, the musical iconoclast. Nothing in my body is harmonious. I am a creature of quintessential cacophony.*

*I don't think Eric cares anything about musical conventions, you say.*

*Then he will fail.*

*Why will he fail?*

*Because, without the hostility of tradition, he will have nothing to beat against. I remember looking at our brown river swollen with runoff from the farms upstream and thinking it a poor companion for serious talk. Tell your friend I bequeath him my scapulae. Of all the bones of the human body the scapula is the most atrociously* dissonant. We walk closer to the river. But in my case the natural formlessness did not satisfy the Creator, or Creatrix, as the case may be. Mine don't match. If your friend Eric were to strike them together percussively and catch that sound, Old Tonality would howl in pain and run away. The world changed utterly. I laugh at my own flight of fancy but quickly sober. I ask if you have a sister.

No. Why do you ask, sir?

Because this man is dangerous to women. You have my permission to laugh. Professor Tyree the troglodyte. Nemo the misogynist. Can never have known a woman. Lacks the requisites. An offensive trace of bitterness sharpens my voice. Is there a woman in his life?

Just his mother. Remember? I saw her with him on the beach. In a gray caftan, like a monk.

Yes, I remember. She's safe. But no other woman will be.

I believe you are right, but I don't worry about Alice. She won't go near him.

Good, but I understand she is often near Deirdre. Intermediaries can also be very dangerous.

Dear Childe Paul, please keep me informed, though I could almost wish your renderings were less vivid. You are mastering the world of the word, perhaps too rapidly for your own good, because such mastery can lead to a dangerous dependency on language. Can you believe that Nemo, the monstrous man of words, is saying this? He says it because the Word will not constitute sufficient protection against Eric, the Anti-Logos. Be careful.

Fondly,
Professor John

* * *

I can't believe how shrunken our lives were. The House of Nordquist ate us up. We forgot everything else.

Or you could say we were totally focused.

How could we be focused? We weren't really together. You were with Eric. I was with Deirdre down in her studio while she painted or up on the hill while she puttered around in the garden. If I was focused on anything it was fighting Eric. It started the day he wouldn't let me come to the tower. And you went along with him.

You didn't miss anything. Everything looked the same out the window. The only thing worth looking at was you down on the ground defying the wind.

Don't soap me up. You weren't anywhere near me. It was one of those times you disappeared into another world. You and Eric sailing the ship into the Arctic.

A gray glutinous substance has attached itself to the window.

OK. But sometimes I thought you were disappearing into Deirdre's paintings.

Nope. Disappearing is your thing. But as for Deirdre's studio, it was like being buried alive. All you could see out of the one round window was weeds. You wondered if you were in a dungeon for doing something really bad. You had to look at hundreds of water colors. Sky, hills, river, trees. Nothing moved. No people. All the birds were dead somewhere. I hated it. You know what?

What?

I like to think of when the flames got to the dungeon of watercolors and melted them into goop and then laughed and burned them up.

Fires feast on fuel. They don't care about anything else. They don't laugh.

I bet you learned that from the Professor.

Yes. He told us about a philosopher who believed that everything has volition. Even a slab of stone.

OK, I'll bite. The stone you and Eric chiseled had the volition to suck up the sounds of a woman's body. But not just any woman's body. The stone was picky. So Deirdre had to go down to the island and find the right one.

Right. The volition of the stone guided my hands when I was chiseling. It guided Deirdre to Helene.

This is fun. The stone is sitting up there on the hill. What do you think it's willing now?

I don't think it's willing anything anymore.

Sure it is. Once you get in the habit of willing things you can't stop. Maybe it's willing that Eric's symphony will be found, and the black book.

Maybe. Anyway, you saved me from the will of the stone.

Saved you? That's a bad joke. You never listened to me.

But you kept me in your eyes. That changed everything.

I didn't want to look at Deirdre or the house or any of that. So all I had to look at was you.

And that saved me.

What are you talking about?

To see in the dark the eye emits a ray of light that strikes the subject, me, and bounces back to the eye of the seer, you. The eye and the brain of the seer register these tiny scintillations like a photo-sensitive film and form them into acts of will. The lookee is struck by spark after spark of light coming from the seer's eyes until the will of the seer overcomes the will of the stone and saves the lookee.

Ha! Ha! Ha! Even I know enough science to know that's bull.

* * *

We're always sifting, always adding and rearranging data, Ms. Albright. I'll let you know if we find anything new.

I hope you will.

Meanwhile, we depend on you to help us. We have a discrepancy in the accounts of how the letters from your husband to Professor Tyree ended up in your husband's desk.

What are the accounts?

One is that Professor Tyree brought them to the House of Nordquist and your son saved them from the fire. The other is that the Professor gave them to Deirdre, who gave them to your husband before the fire.

This is a trick, isn't it? Didn't your lab guys test the letters to see if they were scorched?

Yes.

What did they find?

No evidence of exposure to intense heat.

OK, you want a hypothesis that gets rid of my son?

That would help.

OK, let's say my husband and the Professor were going to make a memory album of old letters and pictures and crushed flowers. There wouldn't have been any locks of hair because the Professor didn't have any. But when the letters and all the other things were pressed together in the album they got hot and started to smolder, like corn at the bottom of a silo. They got scorched. Some of the hottest love letters on record. Your lab guys just missed it.

You have a fine imagination, Ms. Albright. But we have trouble reading them as love letters.

Because you don't often find love pretending to be ideas.

Can we go back to Professor Tyree and Eric's symphony? You said you thought he heard it and it drove him crazy?

Yes.

You think it might have driven him to start the fire?

It's possible.

We have pretty well established that the fire started in Eric's studio and was not accidental.

How do you know that?

The forensic team can tell from the remains of the fire.

Fascinating. But it doesn't tell who started the fire, does it? How about Helene? Maybe she got sick of giving her body and struck a spark off the stone. Is that in the class of the fantastical?

Yes, of course.

My husband had a Professor who taught that everything has volition. So maybe the stone got tired of a withering body and started the fire. Or the wires and the tubes went into open rebellion and started the fire.

But let's stipulate we don't believe that inanimate objects have wills. Then there had to be a human agency.

Right. A human agency, but that's a problem already, because in the House of Nordquist the first thing you have to decide is which ones were humans and which ones weren't.

\* \* \*

The bare ash outside the kitchen window would be invisible if it weren't for a gauzy moon entangled in the leafless branches.

Our trees in the draw weren't this kind, were they?

No, they were oaks.

We went there to get away from the House of Nordquist, but it didn't work, did it?

No, it didn't.

Don't look out the window. There's nothing to see out there. I want you to remember the day I showed you my breasts.

All right. I like that.

Opening my blouse slowly, not saying anything. I wonder how I knew to do it that way.

How did I know not to touch you?

Tell me.

Because your breasts were beautiful and I was afraid.

Beautiful? I looked at them in the mirror for years when I was growing up. They were never beautiful.

Yes they were. I was going to write a poem. I remember some of the phrases. Aureoles suffused with blood . . . delicately ruffled . . . erect in the caress of the warm air.

Why didn't you write it?

I was a little prudish. At college they called me Saint Paul. Besides, I had decided to give up poetry. I wasn't any good at it.

The refrigerator rattles.

That wasn't what stopped you. It was Eric. And Helene lying naked on stone, wire snakes crawling all over her. You were his assistant. Deirdre was his pimp.

Procuress.

OK, procuress. She got Helene for him and kept her alive and started painting the symphony in the book.

How do you know she was painting the symphony? We never saw inside the book.

That's what we keep saying.

* * *

*Dear Professor John,*

*The image of Eric on the beach hangs over the proscenium of my mind like a breeze-wimpled scrim. Pale courser, red hair flaring. Plunging into the river, rising from the waves like some old Greek god. Runnels of water dropping from his impermeable flesh. Higher up at the margin of sand and sedge, the mother waiting in her gray hooded caftan bound at the waist by a white cincture ending in tight fists of knotted cord. Nun or sibyl.*

*I have been feeling the need of some comic relief. The other day it came. Hot as Hades. A delivery truck stopped at the foot of the hill below the House of Nordquist. A curving driveway runs all the way up to the door of the house, but it's very rough and rutted. Eric and I met the truck on the road below.*

*I ain't taking this rig up that road, the driver said, a wiry little man with a face like a rat's, even to the twitching of his nose. And I ain't hauling them crates up them busted steps with no dolly either.*

*Eric stood looking down at the driver as if he might pluck a bolt of lightning from his quiver and fling it into the little man's face. I felt sorry for the driver. I said just get them out of the truck and put them on the ground.*

*OK, I can do that, said the driver, at once relieved and a little abashed. But you gotta sign this paper. He looked at me, then squint-*

ed at the invoice and ran his finger over the letters of the offending name. You Eric Norist?

I took the clipboard from him and signed the paper.

All right. I'll get these things unloaded. He activated the hydraulic lift and lowered four identical crates to the ground. You can do yourself a favor and uncrate them things before you haul them up the hill.

Eric said nothing to that.

You got more stuff coming.

We'll be here, I said.

Can I keep on going down this road and get back to the main road?

I nodded.

Before he pulled away, the driver said, who you plan to bury in them things?

The four corners of the earth, I said.

The driver nodded reflectively. You know, somehow I ain't too worried about that. He drove off.

Working together with hammer and crowbar, Eric and I uncrated four big black speakers and hauled them one by one up the hill, into the house and down to his studio below deck. They look like sarcophagi all right, I said.

Silence.

By the time the speakers were set up in the four corners of the room, we were matted with dust and sweat. We stood silently, still, breathing deeply. Stop time.

There's my little anecdote for today, Professor John. But it wasn't very funny, was it? Not even at the time, Eric hovering silently, bright eyed, like a hawk. Anyway, please don't feel that you need to answer. These letters of mine are selfish, I'm afraid—a way to put into words happenings that would otherwise pass into silence and come back later to vex me. I can't talk with Alice about Eric. All of her resolve is to get me free of him. I'm caught between one I love and one I can't escape. And I'm no equilibrist. Send in the clowns.

As ever,

Paul

* * *

Sometimes, Ms. Albright, you seem to doubt that we will ever get to the bottom of the fire.

My husband would say the fire's a black box. You can keep combing the hill for facts. But the wind has been blowing across that hill every day for twenty years. And the scavengers came after they took the barriers down.

We doubt they took away anything important.

What was important? They wanted a little piece of the story of the weird House of Nordquist. Maybe they have little jars with ashes on their mantel. In lots of movies the ignorant villagers come and carry off treasures, or what they think are treasures.

I notice you often cite movies.

I used to watch old movies on TV, because my husband was looking at a book or walking. But then the boys came and I had to tend to them.

If this story were in an old movie who would've escaped the fire?

Eric?

Your mind seems to be somewhere else.

The ticking of your machine makes me think of the way the reels sounded in the movie house. Did you know there was once a movie house in town?

Yes.

Of course. Your agency researched it. What was the name of it? I can't remember.

The Pantages.

Pantages. Does the name mean anything?

Not that I know of.

Why would you name a movie theater something that doesn't mean anything?

I don't know. But you said that in the old movies Eric would have escaped. How would that be known?

The detectives would use a process of elimination. It wouldn't have been Deirdre.

How do you know?

Escaping wasn't in her nature or she would've escaped her crazy husband and son and gone back to Ireland. As for Helene, it was too late for her to escape again. She had already escaped once, from Germany you said. And the Professor you believe burnt up. So it had to be Eric.

Very logical.

That's the way it was in the old movies, even if it wasn't Sherlock Holmes. You want to know how the movie about the escape goes on?

Yes.

OK. Eric the evil genius is in a high tower over Gotham getting ready to let loose the sounds of Helene's body on the world unless somebody can stop him.

Do you think your husband is trying to find Eric to stop him?

I wouldn't depend on that. My husband was never a stopper. He was more of a watcher. Which is why you don't want your men looking for him.

I'm not sure I follow that.

I mean he wouldn't be looking at something they could detect. They could step into it unawares.

What would he be looking at?

Black box.

* * *

*Dear Childe Paul,*

*I am in receipt of your letter describing your Eric vs. Alice dilemma. I'm writing to remind you of our last conversation. I think it may be pertinent to your current dilemma.*

*We're sitting in my office in an uncomfortable silence. Why uncomfortable? I'll come to that. You're gazing upward, to avoid looking at me I suspect. A small chandelier hangs from the center of a medallion on the ceiling. As you remember, we humanists get offices in the old Hammacher Building, which is slowly decomposing. A piece about the size of a saucer is missing from the medallion. I follow your gaze upward. I'll tell you the story of that unfortunate caesura, I say. One wintry afternoon Professor Tyree returned to his office, having discharged his duty to enlighten the masses with a learned discursus on the "Protagoros." Man is the measure. Looking about him, the Professor beheld a strange sight. Snow flown in through the window and lying on his desk. He approached. He discerned that it was not snow after all but a piece of fallen medallion shattered into many shards. There was a message in that debris. What was the message, Paul Albright, Bachelor of Arts, magna cum laude?*

*Something to do with the impermanence of things.*

*Excellent. The message is you can't step into the same office twice. Heraclitus applied the doctrine of non-repeatability to rivers, but rivers are obvious, even the sluggish snake that crawls through our campus. The Professor had to learn again that nowhere in the world is there a moment of stillness.*

*You say, what if only a minute had passed between your leaving for class and your coming back? Wouldn't the office remain essentially the same?*

*Essentially? I say. Offices don't have essences. Nothing does. We humans may assign essences. They're not in the world. And anyway, a bright scholar like you knows that even during that minim of time during which the Professor was in class new dust has settled on books, which, attacked by mordant acids lurking in their fibers, are continuously yellowing. Change. Inescapable. And now you are leaving us.*

*I had been dreading this moment of leave taking. I think maybe you had too. There is an uncomfortable silence again. I say, what did you think of the commencement address?*

*I thought it was good, pretty standard though—work hard, love your neighbor, seek the truth.*

*Ti estin aletheia? What is truth?*

*You smile. You don't make a very convincing Pilate, Professor. Nevertheless, what was the answer?*

*Jesus had already given the answer, but Pilate missed it, maybe distracted by his wife's dream.*

*What was the answer?*

*That those who listen to the voice of Jesus are of the truth.*

*You've been well taught by the eminent Professor Aptheker, who thinks that Nemo is a footman to the Anti-Christ. But I doubt Pilate was distracted by his dreaming wife. More likely he was just sick to death of Jewish monotheism and Greek logos and longed to return to Roman pragmatism.*

*I don't know what you said at that point. I remember saying, We're surfeited with language. Words. Choking us to death. We don't know how to be silent. Even the priest at extreme unction must speak. Exaudi nos, Domine sancte, et mittere Angelum tuum de cuelis. And does the angel of the Lord come down from the sky to the dying one? Words. You could ask your taciturn friend Eric why he hates words, but that would be self-contradictory, constructing a question from the hated medium to elicit illumination of the hatred. Like starting a fire to learn how to stop fires.*

*You say, speaking makes him so angry that he speaks only when it is absolutely necessary, less and less. Only music can speak the truth. And only his music.*

*Yes. Only his music.*

*And in his music does he retain the sacred numbers of harmony?*

*He denies numbers.*

*Let him deny. He cannot escape both words and numbers. No human has ever appeared in our world so self-denuded that he is unmediated by words or numbers or both, whether he chooses to acknowledge it or not.*

*I'll tell him that.*

*Do, I say. But I was uneasy, because I could not provide you with the talisman that would get you safely out of Eric's underworld.*

*Professor Aptheker was in my office yesterday inveighing against the modern world because it denies foundational truths. Does this put him in the same camp with Eric? No, because the Professor believes that no human can change the world utterly. In the end it will be the Word made flesh that transforms the world. I try to reassure him that I do not deny the Word. How could I deny it? There it stands irrevocably in the text. I only deny that we can have any real knowledge of it.*

*Yours, from Nemo, a yea-sayer in disguise.*

* * *

Are you willing to engage in a little speculation, Ms. Albright?

Sure. I thought that was what we've been doing all along.

Good. Then why do you think Professor Tyree came to the House of Nordquist?

Paul wrote him letters.

None of the letters we have ask him to come. In fact they discourage him.

You have to read between the lines.

All right. Let's take another tack. Do you think the influence of Professor Tyree affected your husband's relationship to Eric?

Probably. He absorbed a lot from the Professor.

What did he absorb?

It wasn't just the words. It was also aura, like what the spirits from beyond have.

Can you expand on that?

The trainer that came to teach channeling said you wouldn't be dealing directly with a person from the beyond. You would be dealing with an aura.

Did you get in touch with any aura?

I was getting one, but I told you I couldn't handle the voltage.

Let's hypothesize that your husband absorbed an aura from Professor Tyree. Could you say what the aura was?

Mostly it was a kind of song, a love song, humming sweet words to make you forget you were listening to an ugly dwarf.

What about your husband's letters to the Professor? Did they have an aura?

Sure. They sang to the Professor to come to the House of Nordquist and save him, because I couldn't.

Save him from Eric?

Yes.

So you think he started the fire to save your husband?

You already asked me, but I've forgotten what I said.

You said if words are flint.

Not very clever, was it?

It was insightful, metaphorically.

You said your husband believed that the fire was an accident.
That's right.

But you disagree.

Yes, even before you told me somebody started it in Eric's
studio. You think it was probably the Professor. But I told you it
could've been Alicia? She hated Eric and she was tired of being
used by Deirdre.

We have ruled Alicia out, at least for the time being. She was
asleep in the cottage when the fire started.

She could've lit a fuse hours before. It's in lots of movies. The
spark crawls along the fuse toward the bomb in the basement while
the millionaire and the swells are having cocktails upstairs.

Nothing leaves more tell-tale clues than a fuse-lit bomb.

OK, that shoots that hypothesis. We're running out of hypotheses. What about Eric?

It seems improbable he would he destroy his own work. I'd
like to go back to your husband.

You think he might've started the fire?

No. His leaving just before we came is suspicious, but he was
in the cottage with you at the time of the fire.

That's what I said.

Why do you think he left after all these years?

There was the phone call.

This is the first time you've mentioned a phone call.

I know I should have, but I like to try to have something new
for these sessions.

All right. Tell me about the phone call please.

It was unusual.

In what way?

I mean because my husband didn't just hang up. The only
phone calls we get are from companies that want to sell something
so we just hang up.

Who was the phone call from?

In the old movies the person with the receiver rolls her eye-
balls around so the audience knows who's on the other end of the
line.

Is that what your husband did?

I doubt it. But I was in another room. You're just funning me, aren't you? Because somewhere out there you've got people listening to every telephone call in the world.

Let's say the call was from an unregistered cell.

I know what you mean. The kind terrorists set bombs off with. Those cells would've ruined a lot of scenes in old movies. The waiter wouldn't have to bring a white telephone to Ingrid Bergman in the Berlin hotel dining room and she wouldn't have to pretend to the Nazi bigwigs at the table that she was talking to her poodle shampooer. A cell would just jiggle in her purse and she would go to the ladies room.

OK. We don't know who called. But whatever the caller said, it made your husband leave abruptly, right?

He didn't leave all that abruptly. I helped him pack because I knew he didn't know how. It was amazing to me that his old college suitcase didn't fall apart while we were packing.

Did he pack anything unusual?

We didn't have anything unusual in the house to pack.

And he didn't tell you what he was going to look for?

In the old movies the wife or girlfriend throws herself around and begs her lover not to go because she knows he's going to his death. The audience can tell from the music and the slanted screen if they haven't caught on to the plot.

But did you have an idea where he was going?

From my husband you didn't get a lot of useful ideas like where he was going. But I know you need to get something on your recorder. So how about going to find a missing person? Or a book? Or himself?

Which seems to you most likely?

Normally I would say a person is more interesting than a book, even if the person is yourself, but of course if the book was paintings of a symphony you could play, that would be special. But I can tell you one thing he's not looking for.

What's that?

My son, who was the one that saved the book from the fire if it got saved. My husband never gave much credit to my sons. He thought they'd been taken away from me before they were born.

* * *

I keep having that dream. A letter swooping up and down in the wind on the hill. I can't catch it. I think I see the word Roman. What do you make of that?

It might be a letter I wrote Professor John describing Eric's practice pieces on the synthesizer.

Practicing for when Helene came?

Yes, but at that time I didn't know about her. Maybe he didn't either.

Sure he knew. And you knew it wasn't going to be you.

Yes, I knew that.

What's Roman got to do with it?

One of the pieces sounded like Roman music—flutes made out of bone and tubas with no valves, just mouthing and buzzing, and brass pans and clappers.

Sounds horrible. What did the other pieces sound like?

One sounded like the sea roaring when you put a conch shell to your ear. Another one sounded like a crackling fire.

Bones and mouths and ears. He was practicing up for when he got a real body.

The kitchen releases small noises, the hum of the refrigerator, the intermittent rattle of the window in its casement, the tinny chattering of a pot vibrating on the stove though there is no fire under it.

Did you write the Professor about Deirdre?

Probably.

What?

I don't remember.

Think of something.

OK, the way the two white balls of the cincture swung back and forth like pendulums.

Like pendulums. That's a metaphor, right?

Yes.

The Professor liked metaphors, didn't he?

Yes.

Think of some other metaphors about Deirdre.

Shadows escaped from the hood of her caftan and slithered along the walls.

Like snakes.

Very good.

Did you write the Professor that Deirdre was Eric's procuress?

Maybe I wrote him that she was one of those dramatis personae that keep slipping out of character, as if they want to be in some other story.

Wrong. She wanted to be in Eric's story and give him everything he wanted. Anyway, talking about slippery characters, did I ever tell you about the time the Professor came by the cottage on his way to find you?

I thought he just stopped by to get directions to the house.

Why would he need directions to a house that stood on top of a hill like an elephant? His eyes were bad, but they weren't that bad.

OK, then tell me.

He stopped a while to pay his respects.

He always said you were my North Star.

He didn't say anything about stars. I got the idea that I was a maiden prisoner in a castle, and you were trying to set me free, which would also set yourself free. You were blowing a horn at the gate on the other side of the moat.

What else did he say?

Nothing. It was all about the castle and prisoner thing. He put in my mind a picture of the master of the castle all in black with a sorceress standing next to him. Eric and Deirdre obviously. But I couldn't see you anywhere. I couldn't hear you blowing a horn. It was weird, but he made it very vivid.

He knew you were trying to get us free.

Maybe, but I was standing up there all in white, a virgin on the battlements. Battlements? Is that right?

Yes.

I know where I remembered that word from.

Where?

From an old movie where Robert Taylor was a knight in love with a Jewish woman. That's the kind of bull the Professor put in my head.

He meant well.

I don't think he ever really knew what he meant.

* * *

*Dear Professor John,*

*I've been reading some class notes that seem relevant to the situation here. They're about hermeneutics. You showed us a picture of Hermes in wingéd sandals and helmet, carrying a caduceus. Remember? Messenger from the gods to men. You challenged us to evaluate the possibility of valid interpretation in an age of skepticism. Butler rose from his seat. I will interpret this desk.*

*Do so, you said.*

*This desk, Herr Professor, is an instrument of servitude.*

*By nature or by deployment?*

*Before we can interpret, said Meachem, we must perform the phenomenological reduction. He instructed us to curl the fingers and thumb of our right hand and make a small telescope. We were to look through it, fixing our gaze on the desk and nothing else.*

*Understand, Mr. Butler, said Meachem, that the desk was only an instrument of servitude while you were sitting in it and while it was subordinated to the Professor's gaze. It must be re-interpreted in the light of its present ontological solitude. How now do you interpret it?*

*Butler was nonplused. Meachem said, may I venture to speak for you, Mr. Butler? The innate construction of the desk reveals its maker's animosity toward the human body, an animosity deriving from a Euclidean disposition to honor only the planar world. Note the imprisoning arm that leaves the scholar only one means of ingress and egress. Note the dull flatness of its top.*

*You summed it up for us. Either we have only the thing itself, in its deskness, in which case nothing more can be said about it. Or we re-embed it in the world and open a pandora's box of interpretations that change from consciousness to consciousness. Ergo hermeneutics as a way to the truth of things is impossible. But you acknowledged that Butler and Meachem had acquitted themselves admirably.*

*I remember that when, following Meachem's instructions, I gazed through the telescope of my curled hand, the desk did really seem to glow with an inner light. I thought if I kept gazing it would give up to me its inner self, though what that would look like I had no idea. Then the animated chatter of the class went on. But I cannot fix Eric with any gaze, telescopic or otherwise. He is uninterpretable, obdurate as stone, stone possessed of volition. I will never win my way to Ericness. Which means I should get out of this story, because the story is itself uninterpretable. But it keeps pulling me in like a maelstrom. And the frightening thing is it doesn't frighten me anymore.*

*A more human quandary. Alice. We are in love, I think. Right now it's a slightly fay kind of love. We're in the woods a lot, but not as lovers. We lean against two separate trees down in the draw and let the distance between us and the intermittent breeze cool our passion. The draw is enclosed in a wall of trees. The blue sky and the clouds above move with an almost stately motion across the tops of the trees. In the subdued breeze Alice's hair lifts and settles as if it had its own breath. We could transform our love into something more human. But would that kill it? One voice within me says you must commit yourself to Alice in a fully human way, or lose her. Another voice whispers that you must keep your love in suspension until the story of Eric and the House of Nordquist has ended.*

*I wish I were walking with you under the arches. I need to hear you speak of these two, even though you don't know them. Eric and Alice. They are too much for me.*

*Please do not feel burdened by this. It does me good just to write it.*

*As ever,*
*Paul*

* * *

I thought showing you my breasts would be enough. It was a lot in those days. But there was Eric.

Someone moves a chair. The floor complains.

I'm waiting for you to say something.

It was more than enough.

Alicia never came to the woods with us. I wouldn't let her.

I never cared much for Alicia. I didn't really believe in her.

Neither did I. But I had to be Alicia in Deirdre's world in order to stay in the story and find out what was going on. I figured it wouldn't cost me much.

What did you do to become Alicia?

I painted myself white and didn't move for a long time and then moved. What do you call people who do that?

Mimes.

I didn't worry too much that the paint might stick.

You were always Alice to me.

Two indistinct faces hover in the window against the darkening tree.

Alice. Alice Coulter. My daddy used to call me by my full name. It had something to do with horses. He would buck me on his knee and sing about all the pretty little horses, black and bay, dapple and gray. But I gave up the name of Coulter. Albright is OK, but not exactly five star.

No.

Coulter was real, but Alicia was not, by its very nature.

Nature doesn't care anything about names.

Right. I didn't think it mattered what name I had. I thought all I had to do was sit by the window and wait for a light to come out of the dark. It didn't have to be an angel. Just anything that would tell me I was pregnant. But the blood always came back. And then it stopped altogether.

I wish it had been different.

During the long silence that follows, the candle's flame brightens the two faces in the window.

I'm not going to kiss you tonight. Maybe I'm never going to kiss you again. What would be the point of it?

\* \* \*

Dear Professor John,

I keep looking for lighter moments that might humanize Eric. One morning the driver came again with his truck and delivered four large crates. Because there was a sprinkle of rain Eric and I did not open the crates until we had carried them to his studio. One crate contained an electronic keyboard, another a metal box with a bank of tube sockets and controls, another a patch board for relaying sound from the synthesizer to the speakers. From the fourth box Eric took out a large packet of tubes, cables and connectors.

Medusa's hair, I said. He frowned. OK, I said, college boy metaphors.

The wiring schematics were labyrinthine. To amuse myself in the long silences while Eric put it all together I worked out an analogy: Eric the Minotaur, Alice Ariadne, myself Theseus. But who was Deirdre? The unnatural lustful Pasiphae, mother of the Minotaur? An unhandsome thought. Who were the sacrificial Athenian youth? How would it work out if you, Professor John, were Theseus?

I went to work at the hardware. Immediately after closing I returned to the House of Nordquist. Mist covered the lowlands and rose up to the foundations of the house like a stagey approximation of ocean waves. In Eric's studio the darkness was broken by a bank of glowing tubes and rows of tiny red and green lights that seemed to be searching frantically for a place to rest. Eric was at the key board. He struck a note. It went from the synthesizer out to the four speakers. The attack of the note was swift, but the decay was so slow that I couldn't have said exactly when the sound ended. I thought about writing a poem about that. I would use the word ritardando. The poem would show that by an act of will one could not only slow but even stop the drift toward silence and negation. But in this story I'm not an ex-college boy poet. I'm Eric's acolyte.

As ever,
Paul

* * *

Shut your eyes and look into the dark and I'll tell you a story about Deirdre.

Good.

Deirdre and Alicia were out on the hilltop. Every day on the hilltop was like every other day on the hilltop. Same wind. Same white clouds rolling across the sky going nowhere. Same weeds waving their heads. Same boring hills and horizons. Same trees in the draw below standing in the same place throwing the same shadows. Same river so lazy you couldn't tell if it was moving. Why are you nodding? You didn't experience this. You were in Eric's studio. Alicia was with Deirdre on the hilltop. She kept hoping for something new. Not the same weedy garden and the same watercolors of the same sky and the same river and the same trees under the same sun.

I get the picture. You said this is a story.

A story. Right. For a story you have to have a particular day. You can't begin a story, once upon a thousand same days, can you?

No.

OK then, once upon a particular day Alicia went with Deirdre to the hilltop. Alicia was an ignorant girl of twenty years or so, none of them worth remembering, yet. Did you catch that scary yet?

Yes.

What do you call that in a story?

Foreshadowing.

Foreshadowing. Good. There were lots of foreshadows at the House of Nordquist. You could say that the house and hill was just one big foreshadow.

You were going to tell me a story.

Right. Deirdre was showing the twenty-something Alicia that everything is made out of Silly Putty though that was probably not what she really wanted to do.

What did she really want to do?

You're jumping ahead.

Sorry.

Alicia had a boyfriend named Paul. He had another name given to him by a professor of words. Childe Paul. Childe does not mean a kid but a noble youth. He had a friend named Eric Nordquist. Actually he was not a friend. What can we call him?

We could call him a workmate.

I don't like the mate part. We'll call them fellow workers. Is that communist?

Not necessarily.

All right then, to this Eric Nordquist, a fellow worker of Childe Paul, the latter was No-Name. How did you like that sentence?

Excellent.

OK, Eric and Nordquist are names with secret meanings. No-Name does not have any secret meanings. You could call this story "The Battle of Names," but that's only one of the plots. A story can have more than one plot, right?

Yes.

How many?

Three or four is usually considered plenty.

Anyway, these fellow workers in the main plot were working on a symphony to change the world.

You said this was a story about Deirdre.

That's right. What kind of name is Deirdre?

Irish.

Irish is not important in this story so we're going to call her The Mother.

OK, just as long as we know who's who.

The question of who's who is part of the story. Are you following me?

I'm waiting for some action.

It's coming. Keep your eyes shut, or you'll get distracted by the animals playing on the wall, pretending to be shadows from the candlelight.

Maybe the animals escaped from that empty wine bottle.

If you're trying to say I've had too much to drink, that's obvious. Nobody would tell a story about the House of Nordquist sober. Anyway nothing is sadder than an empty wine bottle. But to continue. The boyfriend wasn't around Alicia much. He was around Eric, who was at that time playing the part of The Mother's Son.

Was there some doubt about it?

The alleged Mother didn't have red hair.

He got the red hair from his father, Gunnar.

The father is not in this story. Anyway, there are lots of doubts. Who would listen to a story if there weren't doubts. Sometimes there is only one big doubt. Like in Whodunit movies. The only person who doesn't have any doubts is God, which is why nobody puts him in a story.

And why you never see him in the movies.

Ha ha ha. That's the first funny thing you've said in weeks, which is a miracle because you never watch movies. God could be in every movie ever made and you wouldn't know it.

The celluloid God.

I know all about celluloids. It takes sixteen celluloids per second to make a movie no matter how many dead ones are lying on the cutting room floor, which is a famous line about movies.

OK, this story is about The Mother, right?

Right, but we have to talk about Eric, the alleged Son of The Mother. Everything in a good story is alleged until proven one way or the other. This Eric was a true redhead, every hair of his head, his arm pits, his chest, his balls, his legs. I could have mentioned the red hairs around his anus, but it's not necessary for the main plot.

Anuses rarely are.

OK. Once upon a particular day, while the boyfriend named Paul or Childe Paul or No-Name was around Eric, the alleged Son of The Mother, Alicia was around The Mother, and The Mother said something. This was a big surprise because basically up on that particular hilltop there was nothing to say, unless some lost hiker might come by and say, look! Everything up here is Silly Putty. Have you ever seen such a thing? But this particular day The Mother said, in the voice that never went up or down, I'll be going on a trip soon. Now something like that can hit you right in the stomach, especially if all you have in your ears is the wind and insects buzzing around. You know what I mean?

Yes.

I'm surprised you do, because you were around Eric listening to the beginning of the symphony to change the world. Eric is the main character, right?

It depends on who's telling the story.

OK. You have to tell the story of Eric because you were the one who was around him all the time. Think of all the exciting stuff you've got. Not Silly Putty, but a big stone slab, wires, a naked body, coo-coo music and a secret black book without any words in it and one night a talking dwarf down the hall. But to go on. Alicia said, where are you going, Mrs. Nordquist? She put a little snap in the question.

A silence follows, broken only by the sudden sizzle and canting of the candle flame before it rights itself.

So, what did Deirdre say?

That's the end of the chapter. We have to wait. It's called suspense

\* \* \*

*Dear Professor John,*

*I was thinking of you yesterday when I began a poem.*

> *Wind torn clouds like failing traceries*
> *Disfigure the sky's blue vaulting*
> *Where once divinities disguised themselves*
> *As chains of stars and chariots of fire.*

*I wasn't going to write poems anymore. Well, I didn't. Four lines. A misguided attempt to get free of the House of Nordquist, at least for a while.*

*I should go down to the City and get a real job instead of this part-time thing at the hardware. Mollies and lock washers, eight penny commons. But I can't make myself leave Eric. Why? Even I'm not naïve enough to imagine he can change the world. But I feel com-*

pelled to stay here and witness. Where does that imperative come from?

I imagine walking with you in the colonnade. The garden is misty. You say, the imperative comes from words. All your life you've been taught that the way to truth is through words. Whatever we name we possess. But it's really the language that possesses us. Every language has an unconscious. Even as we speak, it's stuffing our heads with hidden mischief. But now comes Eric, the Anti-Logos who refuses to find truth in words. He speaks to you in music and silence, a language you've never heard. Of course you're compelled.

Alice is my other care. I started to say that she's also a captive, Deirdre's Alicia. But that's not true. She's only a captive to my captivity. If I could break free of Eric, she would leave Deirdre in an instant. She's only playing Alicia to stay near me. I don't deserve her faithfulness.

Deirdre has gone on a quest. For what? Whatever Eric sent her to find. Deirdre is as much a captive as I am, but I suspect utterly without reservation.

Dear Professor John, don't feel you have to answer this. It was just a way of resuming our walks in the Cloister. But I'm not sure in my presumptuousness that I put the right words in your mouth. Yes, Eric is certainly the Anti-Logos, but if he were only a spirit of negation, I believe I could break free. I would have Alice's love. I might learn a lesson from Professor Aptheker as well as from you. Love is stronger than death. But the terrible truth is that Eric's music has begun to penetrate more than my ear. I know it's only finger exercises now, but I can tell that it's a prelude to some huge swelling. What if it proves to be a negation, a vast anti-chorale? Can even love free me?

Enough.

I hope the summer is proving productive for you.

As ever,

Paul

* * *

Do you think we should rule out Helene, Ms. Albright?

Yes.

Why?

Because she was very weak at the time of the fire.

You don't have to have a lot of strength to start a fire.

Maybe not, but she'd been pierced a million times.

Pierced by what?

Knives, nails, men. One nail was left in her throat.

Our report says she sang beautifully.

That's right. A nail in the throat makes you sing beautifully. Every note has to get past the iron and the seeping blood.

Did you hear her singing?

If I did, it had to be through the walls. Did you know that iron and blood smell and taste alike?

No, I didn't know that. Chemically they are not alike.

Which goes to show you the human senses are better than chemistry.

Do you think she finally got too weak to sing?

In the old movies the prosecution always says to the witness did there come a time? That's because the witness doesn't remember much of anything so the prosecution has to put the testimony in the witness's blank mind. So you're asking me did there come a time when Helene was too weak to sing? Which shows you don't go to the movies. Singers, divas they call them, are always singing on their death bed even if they're so near the end and cold they have to be wrapped in white ermine. It's a miracle Deirdre kept Helene alive as long as she did. We don't know how.

So you're saying a person could still sing after she was too weak to start a fire.

I'd like to finish about iron and blood.

Please do.

My husband says in our culture of today we have a truncated sensorium. I can't remember all the highfalutin things he says, but I remember that one.

Why do you remember it?

Because if our upbringing had allowed us to touch or smell or taste we could've known from the first who Eric and Deirdre and Helene were.

* * *

*Dear Professor John,*

*Here is a letter called A Prolegomenon to the Phenomenology of Hardware or Getting Away from Eric. Or Childe Paul Bolts from the Nuts. I need to laugh, or at least to smile. Bear with me.*

*Childe Paul's responsibility at the hardware is customer assistance in aisles 2, 3 and 4, 3pm to closing at 6pm. He stands waiting with his County Value apron tied neatly at the waist and his face simulating assurance of rich endowments of hardware knowledge. Nuts and bolts, nails (finishing, concrete, common), hasps, door-stops, shelving standards, washers, mollies, tacks, springs, picture-hanging wire, staples, coils of beaded metal chain, L-shaped brackets, and various esoteric pieces of geometrical metal that nobody hardly ever asks for, so you can ask me if it comes up. That's Old Man Ritter, the owner, speaking.*

*These winter afternoons are long. Childe Paul imagines he will send his prolegomenon to Professor John Tyree at Justin and James College. The work is timely. In every American garage, basement, utility room, closet, and kitchen are boxes, drawers, and shelves inhabited by metallic sprites. At the slightest disturbance they fall or roll along circular or straight paths until the energy imparted by the householder's fumbling hand is exhausted. These creatures are dedicated entirely to Newton and have no understanding that the atomies of their innards have been radically changed by quantum mechanics. They are also ignorant of Pythagoras and the mathematics of harmony. Consequently, the music they make is cacophonous—irritable pings, scrapings, chafing, crochets etc.*

*So here in the domain of the homely mechanical there is further affirmation that Meachem's desk is unknowable. A sixpenny com-*

*mon nail is a self-enclosed entity, obdurate in its simplicity. But it is also a member of a class of similar objects that pierce and bind, and also a member of the larger social order, responding to actions of human agency, which can be utilitarian or cruel. Thus do we quantum age hermeneuts understand that all entities have at once an inviolable interiority and an inescapable social embeddedness.*

*Back to the realities of the House of Nordquist, or the irrealties. No-Name, the acolyte, must assist Eric in the composing of the magnum opus that will change the world. What would Professor Aptheker say? He could not cite a Faustian bargain with Mephistopheles. There is no evidence that Eric wants power. In fact I believe that in the Novus Ordo Seclorum he will no longer exist, having burnt himself up in order to ignite the transfiguration. Anyway, I meet with him early tomorrow morning. I bring from the hardware two heavy mallets, two sets of stone chisels, and two respirators with attached goggles. We wait upon the hour.*

*As ever,*
*Paul, student of farce and bathos*

*P.S. Childe Paul should appear before Professor Aptheker to confess. I have not been funny. I have not told the whole truth, which is that in the bowels of the House of Nordquist, enclosed within walls within walls, I feel an essence aborning. It does not matter that the possibility of essence has been disproven in Professor Tyree's seminar. I feel it. But I cannot ask for absolution because I have no resolve to quit the dungeon and fly to my love, my salvation.*

* * *

Where were we?

You were telling me the story of Deirdre's trip.

OK. Shut your eyes. See those huge banks of snow. Deirdre is in a horse-drawn sled crossing miles and miles of snow. Wouldn't you be worried about wolves?

Yes.

That was a trick question. Nuns never get eaten by wolves. If a wolf gets a nun's wrist in his jaws, he would freeze to death.

The flame of the candle within the chimney gives the appearance of circling around the wick before it settles again into its assigned perpendicularity.

This story is too cold. I don't want to tell it anymore.

What do you want to tell then?

I want to tell the story about my son, the gentlest person I ever knew. I called to him. Don't go back in. I couldn't hear what he answered. Something about saving something. The fire was roaring. What do you think it was?

I don't know.

I don't either. It wouldn't have been Helene. She was in the house drinking flames like wine and singing songs of death with a nail in her throat. It wouldn't be Deirdre either. She was happy to melt like the Wicked Witch in the movie. And the dwarf. Nobody saves a dwarf from a fire. And my son had already saved the letters. So what was there to save?

Eric?

There never could be such a plot, saving a mad scientist. It must have been the book or a tape of the symphony. You might be the only one alive who ever heard it.

I never heard the whole symphony.

You heard everything there was to hear. I don't think it was ever supposed to be whole. Something whole would just play through from beginning to end. It couldn't change anything.

That's right.

Why can't something whole change anything? And don't say black box.

Because to change, things have to be broken up.

Or burnt up.

That'll work.

But the symphony didn't change the world. It just changed your life.

What about your life?

Sure. If it changed your life, it changed my life.

A stillness comes into the kitchen. Their breathing is inaudible. The candle's flame is upright.

After the fire we went down to our trees. But it didn't work, did it?

No.

Why didn't it work?

I don't know.

It didn't work because you weren't there. You've been somewhere else for twenty years. That must be hard, unless it's a real interesting place. OK, you're not saying anything, so I'll tell you what kind of place it is. It's a place to wait. It's like a delivery waiting room in a hospital but the baby never comes.

I wouldn't mind if something happened.

I'll tell you what's happening. Some guy wants to talk to us about the fire. After twenty years. Who do you think he is?

I don't know. An aspiring arsonist.

Not funny. You'd better figure out what you're going to tell him. I'm going to tell him that everything had to burn up so there would be a big mystery and guys like him would have something to do. Maybe that's all Eric really wanted was a big black hole full of mystery without words. How could you make a symphony to change the world anyway? Where would you play it from? The Washington Monument?

Not likely.

Alice tilts the wine bottle over her glass. Nothing comes out. She blows down the neck of the bottle and makes a whooshing sound.

It's not true, you know, that a mother loves all her children the same. The young one was in my heart. The wild one mostly just came out of my belly. When he sent me postcards from dangerous places, I didn't imagine I was hiding with him in the rocks so the savages wouldn't get us. But when I lost the gentle one I tried to dig a hole to bury myself, but the dirt was frozen.

I remember.

You said we should go to a doctor. But what could a doctor do about a hole?

\* \* \*

Dear Childe Paul,

All hail, young lord, who rode to the dark House of Nordquist and blew his trumpet at the gate.

I'm three letters behind. Forgive me. Books, end of semester papers I plead. But nothing is lost. I keep a treasury of your letters. Your epistolary prowess grows. You command a heady mixture of comedy and omen. I will take the letters out of my desk drawer from time to time and bid them sing to me. Words are perilous, as we know, but songs are less so, their syllables disciplined by harmony.

The garden is more and more unruly, you write. Alice and Deirdre weed and plant among haphazard rows. The wind over the hill whistles wildly. The western escarpment severs the sky. The river is fluted with silver ruffles. Sun and moon hazed. The great ship of wood and glass imprisoned in ice. How vividly you sing to me. Poco pesante.

Here only a sullied river, barren trees, the young in their animal spirits and intellectual stupefaction. Around they go, thrice clockwise, thrice counterclockwise. Weave a circle around him thrice, for he has drunk the milk of paradise. No, not paradise. What? The elixir of Logos. But what is the meaning of Nemo's words, words, words? What is truth?

So you report that the machinery of world-changing music is assembled. Cables coiled like a nest of young vipers, red and green lights in a frenetic dance. Four obsidian sarcophagi, paradoxical, tombs for old music, birthing rooms for the new. And all the while the world waits for the Novus Ordo Seclorum. Well, who knows? Eric the Red may do it for us. America was to have given birth to the new order four centuries ago. But we have drowned ourselves in blood. At Antietam soldiers scrambled among the unburied corpses of an earlier battle. Not morituri te salutamus, but we dead, dying a second time, salute you. And there could be yet a third. Who knew that death was repeatable?

I wunder.

Caveat, Paul. You are a dramatis persona in a play not of your own making. Be careful you do not suffer the old American fate of *plunging into an impossible drama: the new Jerusalem, the peace-able kingdom, the triumph of the common man, the celebration of great warriors and protectors of democracy. Behold the grand pa-rades, ticker tape, confetti, motorcades, politicians unburdening themselves of the great rotundities of victory. All drowned in blood.*

*So, with ineluctable music Eric the Red will cleanse us of our fatal myths of nobility. He proposes not a drama of mere iconoclasm. It is not the quarter turn of strophe and antistrophe. It is the ultimate peripeteia, the radical reversal of history, the end of story and music. You have studied enough of the great Greeks to know how such a plot will end. I should say anti-plot. And do not imagine you can revise it. It is his alone. You say you feel compelled to stay by him. Choose your role with extreme care before it is no longer yours to choose. Supernumerary? Witness? Acolyte? Or better yet, exit.*

*As for the poem, it is nicely turned, in the tradition of those who ask after an otiose divinity. Professor Aptheker tells us that in the darkest eras the absence of God is God. That huge black hole turning upon itself is for the remembrance of Presence. How many universes does God have to take care of? In one of them perhaps the sky is luminous. Another savior is born. The mountains are resonant with hymning.*

*Back to Eric and the music of the Novus Ordo. Take care.*

*Look past my undeserving and write often. I have no music but yours. Even the pianissimo of rustling leaves in the cloister garden has died away.*

*Affettuoso,*

*Professor John*

*P.S. I wonder if I myself will be called on stage from the wings? If so, I fear that it means the catastrophe is near.*

* * *

If you had to guess, Ms. Albright, where would you say your husband is?

He's inside himself. But you were thinking about outdoor places, like streets, where you could stake your men out.

Yes.

I'm afraid you haven't been paying any attention to me.

Yes I have, Ms. Albright. You have warned me of dangers, but we need to find your husband.

So where do I think he is? He's looking for Eric.

But suppose it was Professor Tyree who escaped and not Eric.

There isn't any plan B. Anyway, you ask me like my husband and I talked about all these things. My husband had books and beach walks. I had movies and postcards. That was all until I made us sit down in the kitchen and talk about the fire.

Why did you do that?

I don't know. My husband didn't say a lot. Some concepts. Mostly I listened to myself.

What concepts did your husband talk about?

The concept of a symphony that would change the world, or the concept of fire.

Fire isn't a concept. It's a chemical process.

To him it was a concept, about the end.

The end of the House of Nordquist?

That, but also the end of everything. There's a fancy word for the end of everything. He got it from one of his professors, but I can't remember it.

Doomsday?

No, that wasn't it. Anyway you can't find him by following the concepts. They don't leave any trail. Besides, a big concept in the story is missing, his name. Which is a problem for your men because they can't go around knocking on doors and asking if anybody has seen No-Name.

* * *

*Dear Professor John,*

*This time I'm going to try to stick to the story. It's called "The Triumph of Stone." We're deep in the bowels of the house. Eric leads the way with a powerful electric lantern. I carry the stone-cutting tools and the masks. We descend into a dark chamber. The voids, I say. I refuse to be quiet. If I'm going to go down into Eric World, then I'm going down singing, even if it's a song of extinction. I say, if the ship is foundering the captain can give the order to flood the voids for ballast. But it's no use if the ship is locked in ice.*

*Eric says nothing. I used to be able to get a rise out of him, but now almost never. I say, actually the concept of the Void is not very useful. If you sail to the edge of the universe, across many trillions of cubic light years, you would get to the edge of the Void, but to stay on the edge you'd have to keep on sailing at dizzying speeds across huge floods of space-time because the universe is expanding very rapidly. Which is a way of saying that Nature hates a void. One thing, Professor John, about talking to a self-assigned mute is that you don't have to worry about being contradicted no matter how absurd what you say is.*

*We arrive at a metal door. Eric pushes it open. Creaky hinges. I produce a ghoulish laugh. I bet there's a skeleton in here with manacles still around the wrist bones. The hands have fallen apart of course and lie like deformed dice on the stone floor. In the movies these bones are made of plastic because it's against the law to use actual human remains though many families would no doubt give permission in order to get the handsome fees that Hollywood pays for props.*

*Eric hangs the lantern on a big pad eye hammered into the foundation. He nods with satisfaction. In the center of the room is a large granite stone about 6 feet by 3 feet and over a foot thick. It lies on a carefully ordered series of five round timbers. Eric brushes off the surface of the stone. A pallorous cloud of dust rises up in the lantern's light and hangs like an ectoplasm in the stagnant air. Eric motions me to put on the mask.*

*We would make convincing science fiction villains, the filters of the respirators protruding from each side of our nostrils, our eyes goggled. A muffled sound comes from Eric's respirator, maybe words, probably not. With the flat of his hand he motions that we are to smooth the surface of the stone.*

*I nod. Eric takes up mallet and chisel and begins with careful strokes to even out the rough surface of the stone. I join in the work. The stone is less resistive than I would've guessed. Sizeable chips sheer off from the chisel's blade. Even in the slant light now dimmed by rising dust I can still make out the veins in the granite. My hewing gets more effective. The striking of the mallet and the chisel's obedience to task feel good. After a while we change to smaller chisels and work to create a finer surface. For a long time I have remained silent, devoted to the work. Then I remember my vow to talk. When do we start making a design?*

*Eric shakes his head. He means never. After a good deal more smoothing Eric motions that we have done with that phase of our task.*

*Now carefully moving the rearmost timber to a position just in front on the stone, we begin to roll the stone forward. Repeating this repositioning of the timbers in slow rotation we laboriously roll the slab out of the workroom, down the long passageway, and into Eric's studio. There we position it in the middle of the room. We remove our respirators. It feels good to get free of my own stale breath. I almost wonder if it's the heady effect of sudden oxygen that makes me imagine Eric saying, Take your clothes off and lie on the stone.*

*I say, I'll get sweat on it. Yes, we are actually sweating down in the catacombs, where a perpetual clamminess always overrides temperature. Can it really be Christmastide?*

*Eric waves away my compunction summarily. I do as I'm told. The stone is cold. Am I a corpse, I ask.*

*Eric says nothing.*

*A human sacrifice?*

*Eric is standing now at the controls of the synthesizer. I can see the splayed reflection of restless red and green lights in the sweat on his chest and face. The four speakers grumble. I begin to feel the stone drawing the heat from my body. I say, one of our professors told us about a philosopher who believes that nothing is entirely inanimate. He holds that life is an unbroken continuum from stones to animals to humans right up to the angels and God. The lights continue to flicker. You should take an interest in the soul of stones. One brilliant classmate of mine observed that if we acceded to the proposition of ubiquitous consciousness we would have to remain perfectly still. The gentlest caress, even the drawing of breath would perpetrate a fatal cruelty against the tiny organisms that inhabit the air.*

*Eric nods. Whether in agreement with what I say or in confirmation of some unvoiced thought of his own I couldn't say.*

*The coldness of the stone begins to bite. What am I? Give me a name.*

*No-Name.*

*Well, as it turns out No-Name is not to be a living sacrifice. That privilege is reserved for another member of the cast. I'll probably be dispatched at the end of the first act. I should exit now. But every exit from one stage is an entry onto another. I don't remember who said it. I play on several stages—the House of Nordquist, a hardware store, a wooded grove, a cottage. Who am I? Not the one who rode to the dark tower and winded his trumpet, but I thank you for the title. Maybe someday I will live up to it.*

*As ever,*

*~~Childe~~ Paul*

*P.S. I'm sorry to leave you there in the dim light with me shivering on the stone, but I hear the distant chiming of nuts and bolts calling me to duty.*

* * *

Look. The window is making a picture. Candle, wine glasses, fruit bowl. A still life, isn't that what you call it?

Yes.

Still Life with Ghosts. All we need is a dead duck to hang its head over the edge of the table. But who would want to paint it? Not Deirdre. She went straight from kiddie watercolors to painting a symphony in a book, didn't she?

I never saw inside the book. But one time you said you saw inside the book.

I was funning you. But actually we both saw inside the book. We just can't remember it. Like we both heard the symphony, but we can't remember it. Alice lifts the chimney from the lamp, licks her forefinger and thumb and plucks the flame off the candle's wick. It's a trick my daddy taught me. Not something you want to try, though, with a burning house. Alice strikes a match and re-lights the candle. She makes a small space between her thumb and index finger, looks at it carefully and the shuts her eyes.

What are you measuring?

I'm not measuring. I'm seeing if I can shut my eyes and tell the exact second before my thumb and finger touch. They say a blind person has the feel of things she can't see. It's the sixth sense. Maybe that's what Deirdre used when she did the paintings for the book. But the sixth sense wouldn't work in a fire, because the fire is all around you and you panic. That's probably what happened to the Professor behind his Coke bottle glasses. You shouldn't have egged him on to come.

I didn't egg him on. He was a free agent. He did what he chose to do.

You think anybody's really a free agent?

It's something we have to believe to live.

I don't have to believe it. What about Eric? Was he a free agent, or do you have to be a real person to be a free agent?

* * *

*Dear Childe Paul,*

*Winter has no charms here at Justin and James, as you know. No cowl of beautiful white. No hush of new fallen snow. Just sludge and the crackling and dripping of ice. Apropos of your memory of the famous debate on hermeneutics, I declare that this substance outside my window has neither interiority nor social embeddedness unless it's to drive humans to seek shelter together.*

*What should I say about you and Alice? The idea of Nemo as a counselor to lovers would be the subject of spirited mockery here. But I defy my detractors. I declare that there is something between lovers deeper than the chemistry of desire. Otherwise how could love grow in cases of long physical absence? Plato teaches us that love is nascent long before the particular loved one appears, so integral to our being is it. Some would go so far as to say that love is the beginning of everything. That explosive seedling the cosmologists tell us gave birth to our universe brimmed with such love that it could not keep to its boundaries. Still, you're right to ask if what you feel toward Alice is truly love. Because unfortunately there are many sly simulacra of love. It's not safe simply to look into one's heart. The membrane that encompasses the heart to protect it against impurities is alas frail.*

*I will not comment on Eric's drama and your problematical role in it. Instead, I will recall for you a familiar story that I believe pertinent. We are walking our rounds in the Cloister one day. You say you believe that Meachem will become a great success because he is the master not only of words but also of himself. Quite possibly, I say. He will let nothing get in his way. But one day his success will cease to satisfy. It's too easy, when you're as gifted as Meachem, to beat the world at its own game. He will want something else. I don't know exactly what. Maybe he will reach back in time and rescue the old world of origins and essences. I think we need them.*

*What do you think I will become? you want to know.*

*I don't know how to answer. You are at that moment too utterly receptive, like the opening chord of a great piece of music. Everything is there, but the harmonics and the melodic line have only just been foreshadowed.*

*Well, a moment ago I promised you a pertinent story. During the fall of your senior year a famous itinerant artist came to campus, commissioned by the college to create a site-specific work. Remember? One of those so-called conceptual artists that were all the rage, roaming the country nailing down cities, creating fleshly berms of the bodies of enchanted college students, training animal imitators to form themselves into tableaux vivant of the peaceable kingdom,* chalking the moving images of shadows in busy intersections, sculpting the steam rising from manholes, etc. None of us knew what he would do. He prowled around the campus examining every building, every green space, every planting. By the third day of these relentless inspections he had attracted much attention. It's some kind of put-on, Butler said. Many agreed. Probably some Zen baloney. Tomorrow he'll say that he's finished the work, but only those with the third eye can see it.

Meachem did not agree. This guy's for real.

I have to confess that he looked real to me, at least among the frayed realities of our time. He dressed like somebody who really does work, denim and thick boots. He spoke with a strong German accent. His movements were spare and purposeful. On the fourth day he assembled a team of strong students. Meachem enlisted. Butler declined. The task was to scour the woods surrounding the campus for large fallen timbers and bring them back to the green in front of the Science Building.

You and I went out to the edge of the woods, remember, and watched the wood bearers returning with their treasures. The artist dashed about with great verve. He seemed to be everywhere at once, directing his laborers in the selection of wood. Ja, zis ist gut. Nein, zat ist faul.

When a large pile of wood had been accumulated, the artist dismissed his helpers and constructed of the timbers a truncated pyramid. The extraordinary precision practiced by the artist in the stacking of timbers impressed you and me. Butler said, it's like a gross game of pick-up-sticks, only it's rigged so you can't move one piece without moving another one. The case turned out to be very different. The artist climbed onto the pile. No matter which timbers he settled his weight on, the construction stood steady. This feat of stability was demonstrated at an assembly of the entire student body and faculty, remember? We formed a semicircle around the pyramid. Presently the artist jumped nimbly down to the ground and addressed the crowd. Dis pyramid vill not fall. I can take heraus any stueck. He demonstrated by pulling out a piece and jumping up onto the pile again. The construction remained steady. Back on the ground he gave his audience an enigmatic smile.

*Wer hier kann Deutsch sprechen?*

*Professor Aptheker stepped forward. The artist spoke to him at some length.*

*Ich verstehe, said our theologian, and then addressed us. The stability of the pyramid will remain no matter what timber is removed. Except one. The fatal flaw, as in a Greek tragedy. The question is who can figure out which is the fatal timber.*

*As Aptheker spoke, the artist climbed back to the top of his creation.*

*One student stepped forward and with great effort pulled a large timber from near the bottom—an obvious choice. The stack shifted but remained intact, the artist still agilely balanced on top smiling. Not zat von.*

*Another of our muscular lads pulled out an even larger timber. Again the stack moved but rearranged itself quickly into a new equilibrium. Nein.*

*Aptheker addressed us again. You perceive nothing. You are just pulling the logs out at random. Have we taught you nothing about how to study premises and consequences before you act?*

*Meachem stepped away from the semicircle of students and walked slowly around the structure, the artist smiling all the while. Butler called to Meachem, You want to make a bet you can't find it?*

*I thought you, Butler, were the one that said this was all a hoax.*

*I still do. There's no fatal flaw. This is not a Greek tragedy.*

*You're on for a five spot, said Meachem, continuing his examination of the pile. At last he made his choice, a log near the bottom that was undistinguished in any way—size, shape, or position. As soon as he pulled it out, the pyramid began to collapse. The artist had to dance nimbly to get clear of the disintegrating pile, leaping from falling timber to falling timber like a log roller. Reaching the ground safely at last, the pile a shambles behind him, the artist grabbed Meachem's wrist and held his arm up like a champion boxer. Wir mussen dis gross Meister fragen how he know.*

*After a long theatrical silence Meachem said Schopenhauer and walked swiftly away, leaving behind an astonished silence, quickly followed by a great volley of cheers from the groundlings. I believe that you and I joined in. But I remember saying, he should* have said the defeat of Schopenhauer. The pile was not an irrational expression of the artist's will. It was a logical construct, deliberately flawed. Meachem had only to locate the faulty premise.

Word went about that Meachem himself had found the fatal log during the gathering of timbers from the woods and knew that no matter where the artist placed it, the pile would be destabilized by its removal. A great search ensued for this log possessed of black magic. Meanwhile, a great cry went up that the pile must be torched. Some said that Meachem should be burned at the stake as a dangerous warlock, and there was much other sophomoric humor. But the groundskeepers were instructed to take the heap of timbers back into the woods, and the log could never be found. But to this day we here at Justin and James have the expression, a Meachem log, referring to a problem that has a solution, but one that nobody can find. In the Math Department the search for the highest prime number is a Meachem log.

I remember you said you wished you'd been a part of it, gathering timbers if nothing else. I understand that better now. You were already a thinker and a writer. But you wanted to enter also into the world of action, like Meachem.

And now you find yourself torn again. On the one hand, your eloquence is greater than ever. On the other you find yourself in the presence of an actor even more decisive than Meachem and much more dangerous. And you do not know what action to take, or whether to take any action at all. We literary types are inclined to say that the life of contemplation, the life of the Mind, is not only sufficient but holy. Alas, I'm afraid the world will not have it so. The world is always busy about something, though God only knows what and why, and it will punish bystanders. If that is so, you must cease merely to stand by Eric and watch. You must take action, take Alice by the hand and lead her away.

They hand in hand with wandring steps and slow,
Through Eden took thir solitarie way.
And yet the world was all before them.

Your loving teacher in fear and trembling,
Professor John

\* \* \*

I'm happy to report to you, Ms. Albright, that we have a lead in the City.

The City?

You seem surprised.

My husband hates the City.

Why?

He had a professor, not Professor Tyree, who taught them to hate cities. Something in the Bible, about Cain and Abel. He hates crowds and noise and places with lots of glass.

Is this from all that glass in the House of Nordquist?

You got that from my husband's letters, didn't you?

Yes. Also the construction of the house was written up in the *Hudson Wayfarer Weekly*.

I never heard of it.

It went out of business. One of the photographs of the house under construction has an interesting caption. "Is it a house or a ship? Ask the eccentric Gunnar Nordquist."

What did it say about the fire?

It stopped publication long before the fire.

Nothing more about the house in your database?

Yes, architectural details from the county permitting office and the construction company, but back to your husband. What might have made him go to the City if he hates it?

You keep asking the same question—why did he leave, what's he looking for? It's an old courtroom trick in the movies. Mrs. Albright, a moment ago you said that you saw the reflection of the fire in your kitchen window about midnight, but the kitchen window looks down toward the river. Isn't that true? Yes, that is true, sir. Maybe the reflection came off the surface of the water up to the window. It was a very bright fire.

I apologize for being repetitious, but we have to corroborate.

All right then, let's say he's looking for a person.

Who might that be, Ms. Albright?

I'm not trying to be a hostile witness, meaning the prosecution could badger me. The person could be Eric, but we have to stipulate that Eric is a person.

All right, let's stipulate that Eric is a person. Would you also stipulate that the person who started the fire is not necessarily the person who escaped.

Sure. I'll stipulate that. Then what?

That hypothetically means that everybody who was in the house at the time of the fire could have started it. And anybody could have escaped.

What about all of the people who might have gotten into the house at the time?

All evidence leads to the conclusion that the fire was started in Eric's studio by an inmate of the house, not by an outsider.

In the movies that's called an inside job.

We're ruling out all outsiders.

That's about six billion people, I believe, increasing every day, even when there's a killer typhoon.

Do you think we should rule out Deirdre as the escapee? You say that she had a halting way of walking.

I never said halting. Anything but.

Was it a type of walk that would make it hard to escape from a fire?

No. It was a gliding spooky walk. But that doesn't mean it would be easy for her to escape the fire. In the old movies many times the villain gets caught by one of his own devices, like tripping over a wire that goes to the trigger of a shotgun. So Deirdre could have started the fire and gotten her caftan caught in a door that slammed behind her. She would've struggled while the fire caught up to her. She would've ripped the gray caftan so that her thighs showed. This would depend on whether the actress was well endowed as they say, and if Deirdre had thighs. But it would be all to no avail. The fire would burn her up. But I can't picture Deirdre in the part.

Why?

I couldn't say exactly. I only know if I was the chief of casting I wouldn't cast Deirdre as a firebrand.

Do you think there was music like in the movies during the time of the fire?

That's a smart question from a person who doesn't watch movies. Sure, the music always goes up for big tragic scenes. And there could have been offstage singing. That would be very emotional. Helene singing off stage, Deirdre caught in the door, Eric down in his studio trying to save the symphony, the dwarf hobbling toward the door, taking one look back and chuckling evilly. There you have it. Mystery solved. The DNA tests were wrong. Put it in the database. We don't have to meet anymore, much as I hate to lose your company.

\* \* \*

*Dear Professor John,*

*Felicitations at the onset of the new year. Will it be an annus mirabilis?*

*Please don't think I'm ignoring your advice. I haven't quitted the House of Nordquist, but I'm poised to run if and when the time comes. I can't get rid of the idea that there's something I'm supposed to learn from Eric. I'm going to keep writing to you. Maybe you can find something hidden in my words that I can't see.*

*"The Triumph of Stone" continued.*

*I'm still lying naked on the stone. Eric comes with an instrument that looks like a stethoscope. It trails a wire that runs back to the synthesizer. He presses it to my sternum. The speakers report my breathing, my heartbeat. Eric touches my lips.*

*You want me to speak. OK. I'm lying on the bottom of the Arctic Ocean next to your father.*

*Eric moves the instrument down towards my stomach. He signals me to speak again.*

*It's so dark down here the fishes have lanterns for eyes.*

*Eric presses the instrument against my throat.*

*Full fathom five thy father lies. Those are pearls that were his eyes.*

*The pressure of the instrument increases. My breathing is raspy. Ding dong, ding dong bell.*

*Eric removes the instrument and goes back to the synthesizer. I sit up. So?*

*No answer.*

*Nothing?*

*No answer.*

*It was not nothing, I say. I heard the sounds of my body coming out of the speakers. What do you want? I make my voice sly. You want a woman, don't you? Where do you think you'll get a woman to lie naked on this stone?*

*Eric kills the power to the system. The hum of the speakers fades slowly into silence. The lights of the console go out, some more reluctantly than others. Eric tosses me my clothes. I say, Is this the end of my service?*

*No.*

*So, Professor John, we can say I'm safe. By default. Unsuitable as a subject. Merely a member of the chorus. Intensely interested but ignorant. When tragic fate befalls the hero I will cry out with pain and horror, having had only a vague premonition of the catastrophe. That's all. Unless you read something else here.*

*Your foolishly deflated student,*

*No-Name*

\* \* \*

You were telling me a story about Deirdre. I don't remember how long you said Deirdre was gone when she went on her trip.

The walls and the ceiling of the kitchen have receded so that they now return a distant echo. Words attack swiftly and decay slowly.

Long enough for you and me to spend some time in the draw. We could go there now and find the trees we leaned against in those days.

They might be hard to find. You're looking up. I bet it's because you remember the blue sky above the treetops.

I'm looking up because our words are crawling around on the ceiling muttering to each other. The kitchen may be bugged. The agency could use our words for evidence and arrest us.

What would we be arrested for?

Crimes of the heart. We would risk getting caught if we went back to the crime scene. Even just for old times' sake. But we wouldn't be going back just for old times' sake.

What would we go back for?

We'd be looking for something.

What?

For us, the two of us together.

I'd be happy to be there with you.

No you wouldn't. You'd be thinking about Eric. I would see his red hair in a bubble over your head like in the funny papers. In fact I see it now in the candlelight.

What about you? Would there be a bubble over your head?

Sure. There's a bubble over everybody's head.

What would be in it?

My son holding the black book. It's not open. We can't see inside it.

It doesn't matter what's inside it because it's over.

That's what you tried to decide twenty years ago, but it didn't work. You've been waiting for that day when somebody's going to show up.

You mean the agent?

No, you know I didn't mean him, but now that you've mentioned him he'll want to talk to you about the fire.

I'd just as soon not.

OK, when I meet him I'll tell him it's no use asking Paul Albright about anything because he's not much of a talker.

* * *

Dear Professor John,

This will be a different kind of letter. Alice and I are concocting a story of the arrival of the fated woman. We missed her actual arrival, which was at night. We don't want the story of the House of Nordquist to have any holes. Holes in plots are aesthetically and morally dangerous, as you taught us. It's the job of the storyteller to pretend that he knows what happened in the holes. Meachem, our brilliant iconoclast, argued on the contrary that it's the job of the writer to destroy the false narrative that hides the holes.

To go on with Alice's and my story. We've decided that Deirdre conveyed the fated woman here in a black limousine with dark curtains and tinted windows. The vehicle came all the way up the rain-rutted driveway, made temporarily firm by a recent freeze. We couldn't see the driver, but who could he be other than the ferryman of the Styx in modern dress, impeccable mortuary livery, snap-brim leather cap, starched shirt, black tie, black jacket and trousers, black boots so highly polished that they reflected images of constellations, the Dog and the Crab and Hydra. We kicked around an alternate story line. The woman arrived in a fur-lined dory drawn by a team of sharp-fanged huskies. She could see from a distance the ship in the jaws of ice and the bodies of the crew frozen in postures of despair. But she came on. In this version Eric would throw down a Jacob's ladder. He and Deirdre would lift the frail visitor up onto the deck and then take her down to her quarters near Eric's studio, never again to see the light of day, which here in the Arctic winter is not much of a deprivation, the days short and gray, the landscape endless vistas of frozen sea wrinkled by howling winds.

Alice insists that she and I are outside the story. We are detectives. So we skulk around the house at dusk. We peek into the ground level ports. Deirdre's studio is dark and uninhabited. Eric's studio has no ports. We think we hear distant music twisted by the labyrinthine passages that run through the infernal region of the House of Nordquist.

We could of course just knock on the door and ask Deirdre to introduce us to the guest, but that would reduce the possibilities rad-

*ically. Alice says that if we don't find the woman soon we have to give up or we will be trapped in the underworld of the House of Nordquist and bumped off.*

*Maybe later I will have news of the real woman, if there is one.*

*As ever,*
*Paul*

＊ ＊ ＊

Do I know you?

I'm the new guy.

Oh. Well, to tell you the truth I didn't know your predecessor either. He didn't give me his name or number.

We don't have numbers.

Too bad. Something like double oh seven could be exciting. What about me? Do I have a number?

No. We're pleased to know you as Ms. Albright.

You're young. I would've guessed they'd send in a veteran to crack a case like me. Crack a case. You'll hear a lot of expressions like that from me because I used to watch old movies.

I enjoy colorful language.

I think you're going to be different from the other agent, more likeable. Still, I'm sorry if my answers got him taken off the case.

You don't have to worry about that. Rotating agents is standard procedure.

Well he's probably glad to be moving on to someone more exciting. As for standard procedures, my husband and I had one once. We sat in the kitchen many evenings by candlelight and drank wine. But it didn't work. The same questions kept coming back and the answers were always in black boxes.

That must've been disappointing.

Aren't you going to ask me what the questions were?

No. I'm just assuming that you will tell me if you want to.

They were about Eric and the fire. I hope you don't have to ask me everything all over again. The other agent already asked everything twice or more, probably to see if I would give the same answer. I wonder if I passed.

I'm sure you did, but I'm proposing that you and I use a different procedure.

I like the sound of that. How does it work?

I'll just say something and you can respond with whatever comes to mind.

All right.

You have two sons.

This is a sanity test, right?

No, it's just a way for you and me to get started.

OK, I have two sons. The other agent had a lot of trouble getting his head around that.

You decided not to name them.

I know some people find that strange. But I believe that a name given at birth can cause a child's life to be confined or even misdirected.

But the sons did eventually give themselves names.

I'm not sure about that. One died young, it's believed. The other one just signs his cards your roving son. At first I thought it might be loving son, you know an *l* instead of an *r*, but that was just a mother's imagining.

The younger son died in the fire.

That's already in the database. But I have something new to tell. It can be your first scoop. Would you like that?

Yes. I'd be privileged.

In the old movies when a reporter got a scoop, it ended up on the front page, which would go spinning around and around on the screen like the story was a whirlpool that was sucking up everything in the plot. That was the power of news in those days. Nowadays it's a picture of some pop singer with a lot of cleavage who's ditched her abusive boyfriend to everybody's relief.

I'll bet your scoop is real news.

Here it is. I'm thinking about getting a medium to contact my younger son. I have a room I could make dark. Would you happen to know a good medium? I've lost contact with the one I knew a long time ago.

No, I'm afraid not. The agency doesn't use mediums.

That surprises me. In lots of the old movies a psychic might show up at the police station to help solve old murders. Of course some of the murderers were already dead, having lives naturally shorter than most people.

No, we don't use mediums or psychics, but I'll be very interested to hear how your sessions come out if you find a good medium.

In the old movies the detectives can use the words of the returned spirit for clues, but when the case comes to trial the judge won't allow testimony from spirits, because you can't swear them in on the witness stand. So it would be just hearsay.

I see that you are familiar with evidentiary rules.

Do you and I have to follow them?

Suppose you're on the witness stand and I say, Ms. Albright, it is true, is it not, that you have been involved in sessions with mediums.

I'm sure you've heard on the tapes your predecessor made about my failure as a channeler.

Yes.

There was a later time, but it wasn't me that was trying to summon up the person from the beyond. It was a stylist at the beauty parlor who could never do anything with my hair.

You sat in on the session.

Yes. But as I'm sure you know, these sessions are tricky. You have a little heart-shaped pointer on a board. It has to jiggle around and spell the name of the dead one and hope he gets called into the room, usually from behind a curtain. In this case the name of the beloved was Janice, but the pointer spelled out Charles without an *r*. I would've been interested to hear what Chales had to say. Maybe it's a French name. But my friend was hoping for Janice and was too broken up to go on.

That's too bad.

You don't have to worry about me. I'm very stable, even when I'm talking about the son I lost in the fire. And I feel I can talk more freely with you.

That pleases me very much, Ms. Albright.

Thanks. In regard to freedom Paul my husband was an unusual case. For twenty years he was free not to do anything, and then somebody from his past caught up to him.

And then he had to do something.

That's right. But I don't know who it was that called.

* * *

*Dear Professor John,*

*A welcome comic interlude. The rat-faced driver came again. Funeral threads, right? he said. You're going to dress up your victims when you bury em in them black boxes.*

*Eric didn't answer. I helped get the boxes off the lift. Not heavy, but bulky.*

*You two ain't going to put em on yourselves, are you? The driver chuckled. I ain't seen no woman come out of that house yet. Seen a brother once in a hood.*

*We're friars, I said. Celibates.*

*What are you celibating? The driver awarded himself a snuffling laugh, then sobered. I ain't coming here no more. Changing routes. New driver's a woman. Don't look surprised. It's been scientifically proved a one hundred and sixty pound woman can lift anything a one hundred and sixty pound man can, and it don't matter how the body weight's distributed. This one's got muscles big as her tits. The driver flexed his biceps under his heavy jacket. Popeye the sailor woman.*

*We'll see that she's treated courteously, I said.*

*As we carried the boxes up the hill I said to Eric, what's her name?*

*No answer.*

*There can't be two No-Names. I'll be hurt if you take my name away from me. I wasn't sure I'd be allowed to meet her, but I was. To tell you the truth, however, I don't trust my recollection of the meet-*

ing. The afterimages change capriciously so that it gets harder and harder to get back to the event itself. How can one fix an experience so that it exists in a space of its own, outside memory? An oxymoron, Meachem might say.

Anyway, by the appointed hour I had managed to change a charged anticipation into a fixed determination to see the guest as she really is, all context sheared away. Meachem's reductio. And I actually did to a certain degree. I entered the room with confidence. It was not far from Eric's studio, if distance means anything in a labyrinth. Was it cold? No, it didn't seem to me to have any weather at all. I had thought it might have kept some trace of the Arctic voyage. Silly of course, but the memory of the last hours of the ship at the brink of absolute zero will not go away.

To go on, the woman was sitting beside Deirdre on a divan. Actually she was not merely sitting beside Deirdre. She was sitting against Deirdre—shoulders, arms and hips contiguous, but Deirdre much taller, so that if the woman had turned her head, the profile of her face would've been silhouetted against Deirdre's neck. This close proximity made it extremely difficult for me to bracket Deirdre out, but I did.

The room, not large but hollow and echoing, was also hard to bracket out. I'd never seen it before. To start with, the floor presented visual difficulties, parquet laid in repeating chevrons that trapped the eye in a borderless regression. The walls were cleverly painted trompe l'oeil to look like a ship's bulkheads, overlapping steel plates fastened together with round-headed rivets. The ceiling, also trompe l'oeil, simulated I beams and more steel plates. Behind the divan hung a large brown arras in which was woven a baffling moiré that mimicked the repetitive chevrons of the parquetry. I managed to push these vexing appointments into the background but I couldn't get rid of them altogether, the field of vision persistently aslant.

The woman sat perfectly still, face immobile, eyes focused steadily on the middle distance, seemingly on a plane where I did not exist, for she gave no sign of noticing my entrance. She wore a long black gown, sleeves ending at the elbows. These were the threads the rat-faced driver had delivered several days before. Her lower arms and hands were bare. They seemed to me virtually fleshless, the integument a sheer encasement of tendons, veins and bones. The effect, however, was not so much one of emaciation as of an extreme compression aimed at the last degree of reduction just before death. The anatomy revealed within the squared neck line of her gown was congruent— protruding collar bones above a knobby sternum, a deeply shadowed suprasternal notch (I do remember something of my anatomy class). On her head was a tight helmet of cropped black hair. She had dark eyes, pupil and cornea indistinguishable, prominent cheek bones, taut mouth. A fine network of stigmata, tiny livid cross-hatches, scarified her face.

Just as I was completing my mental inventory of the woman's physical attributes, words came from Deirdre. Paul, this is our new fellow artist Helene. Helene has come to help Eric with his music. She's a singer. Helene, this is Paul, Eric's friend and helper. Deirdre's voice was, as always, perfectly even.

Helene's lips parted narrowly like a wound prematurely unsutured. I am pleased to meet you. Every word equally weighted. Germanic accent.

Thank you, I said. I'm glad you've come. I did not say that if a tragic history of pain and wounding was what Eric needed, she certainly looked the part. I did not allow myself to imagine what reductions the black gown might conceal.

I have to go to the hardware now. In the many merchandizing lulls I'll continue to try to fix the image of the woman Helene in my mind just as she was, resisting the distorted afterimages concocted by my predilection toward myth. If I could perform acts of pure concentration not just with the woman Helene but with all phenomena of the House of Nordquist, I might be safe after all.

As ever,
Paul

\* \* \*

I never really got to see Helene. Alice leans back from the candlelight. You don't have to look at me if you don't want to. Everybody's face looks like a devil in candlelight. Sometimes I wish we had just kept on with our game about Helene's arrival. We could've hidden her in a secret room in the cellar where Deirdre and Eric couldn't find her. We could've brought her food and water until the danger was over.

The pretending couldn't go on forever.

I didn't say forever, but you're right. We were never going to beat Eric at his own game, pretending he was going to change the world.

He didn't think he was pretending.

What about sailing to the Arctic? Wasn't that pretending?

No, that was reenacting.

He did it for you, to suck you into the story. He wanted you to look over the edge at absolute zero.

It was make-believe.

No it wasn't. It was real. You were hollering like a Comanche. But never mind. When we stopped pretending, Deirdre sent for me. I've missed you, Alicia, she said. I thought maybe her voice went up and down a little. I asked her where she'd been. I took a trip on a train, she said. I had a hard time picturing Deirdre sitting by a window in her hooded thing, with the trees speeding by and snatching at her face in the glass. Could you picture it?

I never thought about it.

Of course you didn't, because you were down in Eric's studio where there weren't any windows.

Alice makes a gentle huffing. The candle flame sways, a little dance. So you kept going back down there day after day.

I wanted to see how it would end.

I told you it was going to end bad.

I know. And I didn't listen. You were Cassandra. Tell me what happened when Deirdre called you after she came back.

I asked her if she found what she was looking for. She told me she had. She was stooping and scissoring off dead chrysanthemum petals with her fingernails. And right at that moment everything got all blurry except the hand with the nails starting to turn gold from the petals. Have you ever had that happen? I mean everything fading out but just one thing?

Yes.

When was it?

Lots of times.

Name one.

The first time I saw Helene. I did it on purpose.

Why?

So I could concentrate completely on her.

Did it work?

Pretty much.

What about when she was lying naked on the stone?

It wouldn't have worked.

Why?

Because the room was full of things I couldn't make disappear.

Like?

The lights flickering on Eric and the speakers making sounds. What did Deirdre say about her trip?

She said the City was terrible, all sooty and noisy with buildings that blocked out the sun and the air. Everything you hate about the City.

I don't think about the City.

Not even the City of Cain some Professor told you the world was? What was his name?

Aptheker.

It sounds like a medical instrument they use on women.

You were telling me about Deirdre's trip.

Deirdre said, you're young, Alicia. Embrace your lover. I told her I didn't have a lover. She said, I want you to take my hand, Alicia. My hands are chilled. Your hands are always warm. I need their warmth. I want you to walk with me to the edge of the garden. I want to get the hills and the river back in my eye again. So I walked with her. There was a barge on the river with a little tug pushing it up against the wind and the current. It was hardly moving. I couldn't see anybody on the decks. It could've been a ghost ship like the ones that come out of the fog in the old movies.

Is that what were you thinking?

No. I was thinking she never would get the hills and the river back in her eye like before, or paint those childish watercolors again. How do you think I knew that? And don't say black box.

You detected a change in her voice, something in her eye. You could always see things other people didn't see.

That's called a seer, right? I felt the chill in her hand. I could see she was changed. But seeing is a curse. Nobody listens to you. Guess what I'm seeing now.

What?

Journeys. You and I are going on journeys.

Where are we going?

Different places.

\* \* \*

*Dear Childe Paul*

*This may help. Consider the possibility that anteriority is what you experienced with the woman on the divan. I got this concept from Aptheker. At first I thought he was saying alteriority, which I was familiar with—a high degree of difference. That also would fit your experience: the woman Helene sitting beside Deirdre, black vs. gray; thin vs. full. But Aptheker was saying anteriority, a theological concept, he said, derived from ancient debates among Christologists. Was there one person in Christ, an indivisible amalgam of the divine and the human, or were there two? If the latter, then at any given moment of the Gospel story one identity achieves anteriority while the other recedes. Jesus the son of man weeps. The Christ of the Godhead knows, without seeing her, that the woman is touching his robe.*

*In the old days Aptheker and I used to argue fiercely about the nature of narrative. He held that every story was either anagogical, an episode within divine revelation, or was a denial of the divine, in which case God at the time of the judgment would hurl it into the pit. I held that stories begin as autonomous inventions and then willy nilly reach out into the world and shape it. And visa versa, a*

*constant dialog between invention and reality. Etc. The administra-
tion encouraged us to make our contentions public. The Admissions
people loved it—come to Justin and James and witness the famous
debates between the profound theologian Aptheker, son of Martin
Luther, and the clever Sophist Nemo Tyree. Can you imagine such
a thing having any appeal to students nowadays? Anyway, the two
of us still argue, passionately if not publicly. For Aptheker I'm the
Chaos he must shape. He's the Stone I must break.*

    *You, Childe Paul, are the student I could not bear to lose. But
you know that. And you know how worried I am about your fascina-
tion with Eric Nordquist, the very name cold and twisted. And now
the weird Helene of Aptheker's anteriority. Your forceful eye brought
forward one identity and disciplined itself to focus on that, but what
other identity lies within, to be called out into a different perhaps
fatal anteriority? I tell you, Childe Paul, I know this woman. She's a
living fragment broken off the history of our nightmarish century. I
predict that Eric with his machine and his manic determination and
self-honed skills will extract from her a testament of suffering more
horrible than anything you or I could imagine. That's what the feverish lights and serpentine coils are, instruments of a male succubus
fattening on a sacrificial body already reduced by barbarism to skin
and bone, the face a palimpsest written over by war and genocide.
Deirdre will have to keep her alive until the ghastly exchange is complete. Think, Childe Paul, what more may be revealed on the cold
stone. Do you insist on witnessing that?*

    *Perhaps someday I must come to the House of Nordquist. In my
mind's eye two rivers diverge. One flows just down the hill here with
its history of cattle and corn. Narrow, turgid and godless, tamed and
stained by man. No courser of alabaster flesh and fiery crown will
ever appear on its shore. For that you need a river like yours, not a
slavish tributary but a strong river with its heart seaward. In a hap-
pier time it could have given birth to a true hero, a maker of noble
music. But in this age it has spawned a destructive iconoclast. The
corruption of the best is the worst. Son of a father who thought he
could sail to the edge of the void and look down. But his mind broke.
He left behind a son who would seek the opposite, a searing music, an
absolute fire out of which would rise the Phoenix of a new creation.*

*Good-bye for now, Childe Paul. I long to see you. I long to meet Alice, your true north.*

> *Yours in anticipation and love,*
> *Professor John*

* * *

My name is not important, Mr. Meachem.

All right then, perhaps you can tell me who you are in a more generic sense.

I represent an agency that is looking for Paul Albright. You made a telephone call to him on May 12, about 8pm.

Yes, that sounds about right.

Why did you call him?

It was time for us to renew our arguments about the deconstruction of the self in the modern world. It had been a quarter of a century.

Our records show that all you left was a number.

That's correct.

Can you tell us what the number was, and its significance?

I'm not prepared to talk about the number at this moment.

All right then. We have reports that he came here.

Yes, he did.

Do you know where he is now?

He's not hiding in the garden.

I was just admiring your plantings.

Ferns, hosta, daylilies, pampas grass, bellflowers, a climbing clematis. Not my work but the work of my gardener.

I'm not much of a horticulturist.

Everything in a garden has significance. An agent that can't read gardens is at a decided disadvantage.

The case at hand has nothing to do with gardens.

Sooner or later it may.

Did Paul Albright reveal to you why he left home?

Not precisely.

But you have an idea.

I believe he left because of a sudden urgency.

What was urgent?

He remembered a fire and its antecedents as if it were yesterday. The twenty years since its occurrence were erased on the instant. He believes a survivor is waiting for him.

Did he regret his delay?

No, I don't think time matters to him. Everything is present. A passionate intention lying dormant for twenty years has burst forth like an overnight crocus.

So he came to you because he thought you could help him find this person?

He came to my garden. Let me describe my gardener. Five feet tall, a hundred pounds at the most. Blue veins, skin like old meerschaum. Silver hair, hat woven of fibers sanctified during the Tokugawa Shogunate.

What does he have to do with Albright, sir? He sounds like a typical Japanese gardener.

He's archetypical. No doubt you encounter many archetypes in your line of work.

We don't use that classification.

Well, by whatever name, archetypes can be, as you surely know, dangerous.

As an agent I must attend to all things relevant to this specific case. If gardens and archetypes are relevant, I will consider them.

Excellent, because Paul Albright is in search of an archetype.

What archetype is he searching for?

I hesitate to say. The misidentification of an archetype will have serious consequences. Albright himself is an archetype.

I appreciate your concern. But we have to work with all data relevant to the case. We have to formulate working hypotheses, however speculative.

Have you formulated a hypothesis at this point?

Several tentative ones, based in part on interviews with Albright's wife.

Alice. I've never seen her. Another archetype maybe. Has she been helpful?

Yes, though she has never been able to satisfy herself about the causes of the fire.

Fire. There's an archetype par excellence for you. Are you investigating the fire?

Yes, and all the circumstances surrounding it.

Do you hypothesized that the criminal or criminals are still at large?

We're not interested in crimes.

What are you interested in?

The conversion of mystery into data.

Ah. Then you follow a long tradition of thinkers for whom the eradication of mystery is a necessary condition for the reign of rationality.

I'm glad you understand that, sir. It makes me confident you will help us.

I will help if I can, but I would feel more comfortable if I were sure you understand the particular dangers involved in this case.

You're referring to the archetype that Albright is searching for?

Not exactly. I'm referring to the places that Albright is creating in his search for the archetype.

I'm not sure what you mean by creating. Everybody enters and exits various places. We follow them. Do you mean Albright's hiding places?

He has no interest in hiding. It's not his hiding that makes your search dangerous.

What makes it dangerous?

His places are not the kind of places you are accustomed to.

What makes them so different?

Several things. To start with, there's nothing between them.

If there's nothing between them, then they're all one place, which simplifies things.

What you say is perfectly logical, but erroneous. Let me propose a hypothetical situation.

Go ahead.

Suppose I get up from my chair and disappear. A moment later you see me under the trellised archway leading into the garden. I disappear from that locus. Now you see me out in the garden. I disappear. Maybe, you think, I have lain down among the flowers. Or is it possible I have crawled into the little wooded area beyond? Weary of these irritating concealments, you manage to leap precisely into the place where I was last seen. What happens?

I miss you or I seize you.

No you don't.

What do I do?

You disappear. I reappear seated here on my chair.

Where am I?

I don't know, but I don't expect to see you again.

Is this a conundrum to get rid of me?

Not at all. My door is always open. I'll be happy to see you any time. It will be reassuring.

\* \* \*

It was not just . . . what was the word you used? Aberrant, aberration?

I don't remember saying it was.

Who else would've said it?

A character in one of your old movies.

Could be. Some sharp evil guy, like Claude Raines. Anyway I'll describe it again.

You've already described it quite well.

I'm going to describe it again. Something new might come out. We were in the garden, but Deirdre was standing up very straight. I don't know why. Maybe she needed to stand up straight so she could see over the gray Silly Putty that was all around. I never could. Not tall enough. You following me?

Yes.

She wasn't doing anything. She wasn't saying anything. Then it came. It was like a mirror turning on a spindle on a dresser in the baroness's boudoir in an old movie. But when the baroness looks in the mirror she doesn't see her face, she sees a skull. So you know somebody is going to come up behind her before she can take her pearl necklace off and strangle her with it.

Is this is a story about Deirdre trying to strangle you?

Don't be a wise-ass. This is when the thing came like the mirror I'm trying to get you to see, slowly turning. It went from a thin slice to a circle, but nothing was reflected in it.

Very strange. Where did you say you saw it exactly?

I didn't say where I saw it exactly. If I had to say where it was I would say it was under Deirdre's caftan, but if it was under her caftan I wouldn't have seen it, right?

In dreams occluding surfaces are easily penetrated.

It wasn't a dream. It was up on the hill in broad daylight. OK? OK.

What's the use of a mirror with nothing in it?

When vampires look in mirrors they can't see themselves.

Where did you get that? You never watch movies. Anyway I have to see what's in the mirror or I can't go on with the story.

Then stipulate something. You can always change it later.

No you can't. Remember in the movie Humphrey Bogart the defense lawyer is willing to stipulate that the kid was in the house at the time of the murder, and then he can't take it back when the kid claims he was with the girl in the old deserted warehouse.

All right, how about this? It was a reflection of Deirdre's body.

OK, let's pretend it was a reflection of Deirdre's naked body. What would you expect? A beautiful body, like a statue?

I never tried to guess what Deirdre's body looked like.

Let's pretend you did guess. You guessed it definitely was not beautiful. Thick calves, a big round belly like pregnant almost, a big shelf of a butt, fleshy upper arms. What were the breasts like? Were they like mine?

This is your story.

It's both of our story. Heavy breasts with big dark tits like they were full of milk. What do you think?

Perfect example of a Celtic body.

I don't know anything about Celtic bodies, so I couldn't have guessed those details, right?

Right. So where did you get the details?

Let's stipulate you went to Eric and asked him if he ever saw his mother's naked body in a mirror that didn't reflect anything.

I decline to stipulate that. I wouldn't ask him any such thing. Stories have to be believable, at least according to their own premises.

The premise here is we need another witness. The prosecution can't rely on just one witness. The occurrence has to be corroborated or the jury will doubt his theory of the murder. There's always one juror who won't believe anything unless it's shown at least twice. He smokes lots of cigarettes in the jurors' room and all the other jurors hate him. They sit at the other end of the table from him. The warden stands at the door breathing all that secondhand smoke. He hates them all, but he hates the hold-out the most.

An interesting scene.

I think it really was Deirdre's body. You know why?

Why?

Because what I was looking for in the mirror was a picture of what was going on. So one natural place to look for it was in Deirdre's body. Right?

This is your story.

You ought to know if anybody does what I mean about looking in a woman's body. You and Eric looked everywhere in Helene's body for the right sounds. Right? Did you find them?

I'm not the one who decided if the sounds were right. Besides, the symphony's gone.

Eric had X-ray ears, didn't he? He could hear down into the brain and lungs and stomach. And the bones beating on the skin. Bum, bum, bum. What kind of music does the vagina make?

I don't know, but I can tell you the body is never quiet anywhere.

What about burnt up bodies? What kind of music do they make?

Eric didn't compose with burnt up bodies.

You wanted to be the body on the stone, didn't you? But then you would've had to be a burnt up, right? Because according to the premise of the story Eric had to use everybody up and then burn them.

If that's the way it was then I was lucky not to be the body.

What about Deirdre? Did he ever give her body a shot at being the symphony?

No. Of course not.

Why of course not? A symphony of incest. Couldn't that change the world? What about that big Greek incest play you told me about? Didn't it change the world?

I don't think so.

I bet Deirdre wanted to be the body on the stone, even if she had to be burnt up. She wished she could go down to the island and find herself. Then she could moonlight. Lie on the stone during the day and paint the symphony at night. Is that believable according to the premises?

No.

Let's move on to the Professor. I bet his body would make some interesting sounds, but he couldn't be used even as a second stringer.

Why?

Because he couldn't lie level on the stone unless some heavy object, like another large person, was used to press him flat.

The room is suddenly quiet, the flame of the candle still.

I'm sorry I said that. It was cruel. I said it out of spite. He loved you. When two people love the same person there's always spite.

You were telling the story of looking for something in Deirdre's body.

That's right. Her body knew what was up even if her head didn't. But I couldn't get the mirror at the right angle to see it.

You didn't need to. You already knew what was up.

Is this that Cassandra thing again?

Yes. But it's a sad story. I'll try to think of one with a happy ending.

* * *

Well, sometimes we don't nail it right away, Ms. Albright. We build up data to narrow the possibilities. Sooner or later we come to such a high degree of probability that we have certainty.

That's exactly what your predecessor said. I admire consistency. But I can't help feeling sorry for the narrowed out possibilities. They've probably got interesting stories of their own.

You're a generous person, Ms. Albright.

Anyway, you say it nicer than the other agent. He was big on ruling out improbables. Zap. Zap. A method Paul might go for.

Paul sounds like a man of purpose.

That's right. Wherever he is he's got his eye focused right on something until it's not where it naturally used to be, and everything else is erased.

We believe he has a lead.

What kind of lead?

A number.

He's not a numbers person. He's a words person. He'll have a lot of trouble finding the right number.

We believe it's possible that the number could be an encryption of an address.

That's interesting. The other agent was good at numbers. He could number human remains, but I could never get it straight. DNA matches and all that. It was over my head.

Numbers are usually helpful in our line of work.

I like your way of not asking questions. It opens things up.

I'll bet you know the number Paul was looking for in the City.

See? Whether you're right or wrong, it gives me a chance to say my piece, which is I don't know the number. But I know how a good detective could find out.

Please tell me.

Paul got the number on the phone and wrote it down. He took the paper with him, naturally, but you could find the page under where he wrote it. You could use gun powder and bring up the number from its dints. I saw it in a movie. The Gestapo found a number that way and tracked down Charles Boyer and killed him.

I'll bet you also know who the caller was.

I couldn't even guess. But now that you've got me started on numbers, here's an interesting one, two hundred and three. You know what it is?

No.

It's the number of bones in the human body. You'd think it would be even, wouldn't you, God being evenhanded according to one of Paul's professors. Anyway, after the fire I got interested in anatomy. It was morbid, but I couldn't help it. I wondered how many different musical instruments Eric could find in a body. The bones you could put in the drumming section. The muscles and tendons could be put in the string section. But after that it got too much for me. The circulation system and the heart and lungs and stomach not to speak of the pancreas and the urinary track and the optic nerve and so forth. I gave up. But I bet Eric got all of them on his machine.

Of course we can't tell anything about that from the remains.

Could you go over the remains again? The other agent told me, but I got sidetracked thinking about my son.

Happy to do it, Ms. Albright. We have identified the remains of three distinct victims, two of which we have been able to get DNA from. The DNA of the two we have don't match. We have not been able to find, other than the remains, DNA samples for any of the three victims except possibly a tentative match for Professor Tyree. So, of the four in the house at the time of the fire, one escaped. We don't know which one. We think probably not Professor Tyree.

Thank you. And don't worry. I'm not going into the story of my son again. It's no doubt already in your records as evidence that I'm crazy.

We wouldn't be talking to you if we thought you were crazy, Ms. Albright.

Probably you would. Detectives have to talk to anybody, and sometimes it's the babbling old boozer that drops the clue that lets Humphrey Bogart solve the mystery. He doesn't think it's important at first, but back in his shabby office he lights a cigarette and his eyes go inward and it clicks and he jumps out of his chair. But motherhood is not the kind of mystery Bogart could solve. I don't think it will ever be in your database.

I can assure you that your motherhood is in the database.

Who would've guessed? In the movies the judge can say strike that from the record. I bet you have experts striking stuff from the database.

No. Everything goes in and stays. We may reclassify, but we never delete. Back to the fire, we understand there were strange things going on at the house at the time.

Which makes me wonder who you're talking to besides me. But, yes, there were strange things.

Please tell me.

Well, like Eric's hair was growing long, like a witch. It looked like his head and shoulders were on fire. What do they call male witches?

Warlocks.

Helene was getting thinner and thinner, Paul said, until you could've counted all two hundred and three bones. Actually he didn't say the number. He wasn't a numbers person.

Deirdre on the other hand seems not to have changed much.

She did change, but it was hard to see. She stopped painting kids' watercolors and started painting the symphony in the black book you think you're going to find some day. She kept Helene alive and brought her to Eric's studio every day. But she just kept gliding and talking in a voice that never went up or down. The change was deep inside. I can't explain it.

Interesting. You're right about the book. We do believe we have good prospects of finding both it and Paul.

I wish I had good prospects. Sometimes I feel like I'm living in a fog, or I am the fog.

You're anything but foggy, Ms. Albright.

Thank you. That made my day.

To go back to the changes in people. Professor Tyree seems to have been the most changed of all.

I never saw him after the first day he came to the house. But I have it in my mind that he heard Eric's music and it tipped him over. Except if you look at that last letter he wrote Paul you could say he was already tipped over or about to be.

We understand you heard fragments of Eric's music though you were never in his studio.

Did I say music? Whatever it was, I don't think I heard it in my ear. It was more like I felt it in my bones coming through the walls and floor of the house.

One of our tentative hypotheses is that Professor Tyree started the fire to save his beloved student. A question, though, is whether he was capable of it.

I told you I only saw him once, but a dwarf sticks in your mind. He didn't look like a firebrand to me, especially with that little black thing on his head like his brains were soot, but people can fool you.

\* \* \*

The window is an abstract, so evenly balanced are the soughing ash, the candlelit faces and the imperfect transparency of the glass.

Did I tell you the story of the paintings?

No.

One particular day Deirdre called Alicia to her studio. I want to show you something, she said. It was a watercolor on a thick page in a big sketch book. It weirded Alicia out the minute she saw it. You need to ask me why, because I'm having a hard time telling this story.

Then tell something else more probable.

No, I need to tell this, because the painting must've been the first one in the book of the symphony that escaped the fire.

Do we know the book escaped the fire?

We don't know for sure, but by the time I finish we might.

OK. Deirdre showed you a painting in the book.

By the end there must've been lots of paintings in the book, right?

I never got to look in the book.

You didn't have to look in it. There was Eric standing not ten feet from you looking and turning pages, right? So, the prosecution says, did there come a time when you surmised there were a number of paintings in the book?

Yes.

Would you surmise there were, say, six paintings? No, you say, because six isn't an important number.

Actually six is an important number.

Really? What's the importance of six?

It's the number for two interlocking triangles.

What do two interlocking triangle do?

They stand for symmetry.

Alice leans into the candlelight. Her face resembles a clumsily made mask, unevenly shadowed. You're not a numbers person. You're making this up.

No, it's regularly in books about the occult.

Occult. Like Ouija boards?

Yes.

OK, what if the prosecution said, would you say there were five drawings? Is that an important number?

Yes. Five is a quincunx.

What's that?

A geometrical shape of five things.

What things?

Any things that are hard to balance.

Five. Hard to balance. Ha. I get it. Alice.

Alice?

Alice. The name Alice. It has five letters.

You're not unbalanced.

Sure I am. Alicia has six letters. See? Deirdre was trying to change me from unbalanced to symmetry. But I never wanted to be symmetry.

I don't believe Deirdre was thinking about numbers.

You're not supposed to believe anything about Deirdre. I was the one who was around Deirdre.

OK, I don't know what Deirdre was thinking about.

Tell me what you think Deirdre was thinking about, even though you're wrong.

Deirdre wanted her own version of you. Alicia is more elegant than Alice, more European and sophisticated.

Alicia wasn't sophisticated. She stayed around Deirdre and did what she was told. She could've stopped at any time, but she wanted to know what was going on, especially after Helene came. That gave Deirdre power over Alicia.

Do you think Deirdre knew everything that was going on?

We were talking about my names.

Right. What's in a name?

When you frown like that the candlelight makes it look like you have two mouths.

It would be the same if I smiled. You were going to tell me a story of the day Deirdre called you in to see a painting.

I told you I'm having a hard time telling it.

Why?

Because my son died getting the book out of the fire.

Do we know he got it out?

We don't know anything. But I believe it got saved and my son died trying to save it. That's a paradox. You know who taught me that?

No.

You. You want to know another paradox?

Sure.

You don't think you saw the paintings but you did. Maybe not with your eyes but with your sixth sense. The book was right there in Eric's hands.

The flame of candle has burned low. It looks pinched and faint.

Who has the book now?

I didn't say anybody had it.

OK, where is it?

That's not in this story. The story is about Deirdre's painting.

All right, tell me the story of Deirdre's painting.

OK. In the studio Deirdre said, what do you think of it, Alicia? Alicia was weirded out. Alicia asked if it had a name. No, it will never have a name. Alicia didn't know what to say. Deirdre said if you paint something as it is, then that's all it is. But you can paint it from the inside. Alicia looked closer. It looked like it was once part of a body, but somebody had changed it, maybe five or six times. The change was that sometimes it was full and sometimes it was wrung out. When it was wrung out it was twisted, like the Professor, but either way you could guess what it used to be. What do you call that when you can see two different layers of a picture at once?

A double image or a palimpsest maybe. Who was it when it was full?

I didn't say it was anybody, but if I had to guess I would say it was Helene, but I don't have to guess. Alicia said she needed to think about the painting. Deirdre said to come back and look whenever she wanted to. And there would be more paintings, maybe five or six. Alicia said she didn't need to come back because she had the painting in her head and could keep looking at it. If you had said that, it would be true, wouldn't it?

Why do you say that?

Because when something gets in your head it doesn't go away. Is there a name for that?

Eidetic. But I'm not eidetic.

Never mind eidetic. Deirdre told me she'd been thinking of painting me. But she had to keep painting for Eric. I'm glad she never painted me.

Why?

It's a primitive thing. If somebody makes an image of you, they can do whatever they want with you. Or you could suck the sounds out of somebody's body and make it sound like whatever you wanted to. I didn't want my body sucked up in Deirdre's paintings. See? Alicia and No-Name. Nothings. We could've gotten free from all that. But we didn't, did we?

* * *

*Dear Professor John,*

    *I have all the notes I took from your class and all the papers I wrote for you. A pack rat. I've been rereading some of these lately. I keep hoping that if I recapture those wonderful memories, they can unchain me from Eric. Anyway, here's an excerpt from something I wrote and you praised. It may seem to you an odd choice for my purposes. I won't try to explain.*

> *The streets of the city reek of death.*
> *Woe to you women in labor.*
> *Your children will be stillborn.*
> *The blood of birthing cannot be stanched.*
> *Who has brought this plague upon the city?*
> *O King, entreat the gods to reveal the source of this corruption.*
> *How can we cleanse ourselves?*
> *Water writhes on our lips.*
> *The earth sucks at our feet.*
> *The sun burns the air.*
> *We cannot breathe.*

    *Your praise came when we were walking in the cloister. The garden was fallow. The trees were almost barren. What leaves were left had been bitten by the first frost. You stopped and looked out into the broken light. My life has fallen into the sere and the yellow leaf. You laughed but it was a dry laugh. What a destiny, you said, to pursue the search for one's identity no matter where it leads. Then there in the chill of the late autumn stones I asked, What's the difference between one's identity and one's self?*

    *Ha. If you and I could answer that, we would be in the Sheldonian Theatre at Oxford on the occasion of the Encaenia. Degrees of Doctor of Letters, honoris causa, for Professors Paul Albright and John Tyree. A fulsome citation would be intoned. These thinkers nonpareil, navigating the treacherous waters of positivism on the one hand and relativism on the other, have in their great* Prolegomenon to the Sovereignty of the Self *established the very grounds upon which we may know what and who we are.*

*We laughed together. But you went on, suddenly serious. What must we do with our identities, Paul? Clasp them to our breasts? Be true to them all our lives? Or curse them as a prison of false consciousness imposed by society on the true self and so commit ourselves to struggle against them all our lives? What profiteth a man if he gain the whole world and lose his self?*

*I said (I don't exactly know why), This is crazy, but I wonder if we all secretly yearn to be notorious criminals, killers of our fathers, lovers of our mothers.*

*Not so crazy. Look up. These fragile arches above us, we know, cannot protect us from the Furies. We cry out in chorus that we have murdered no one, have not coupled with our mother, will bring no plague on our city. Here, we say to Oedipus, take upon yourself our piddling sins and our drab fates. Perform for us murder and incest. Blind yourself so that we can see. Yes. But what does Professor Aptheker say? Oedipus' eternal infamy was never a sufficient sacrifice. He's off in Colonus, dwindling into oblivion. We always had to have the Christ.*

*But I didn't want to be in need of an Oedipus or a Christ. My mind veered away from you and Professor Aptheker. I saw Alice's head rising above the brow of the hill, coming toward me. Her hair would reach me first, soft little whips lashing my neck. She would be smiling. I would kiss her. Then we would go down to our favorite trees, sheltered from the sky, and talk. And then we would stop talking. The high whistle of a bird in flight would come down through the treetops. Beneath the trees squirrels and chipmunks would scamper from posture to posture, like children in a game of One-Two-Three-Freeze.*

*At that moment my memory of the forest was more vivid than the cloister we were walking together, Alice's face more vibrant than the faces of those that passed by us. Her hair, quiet at last, was pinioned against the bark of the tree or curled tenderly against her neck. Her gaze was at once soft and piercing, her head cocked a little. I imagined she could detect the slightest change in the knocking of my heart. The river was out of sight, of course, but in my mind's eye I could see the curl of beach along the little bay. Part of me was always there, even as I looked at the beloved face of Alice, waiting for the flash of fire to cross the beach again, brightening the air and plunging, inextinguishable, into the dark water.*

*You said, I won't ask what you've been thinking about in this long silence.*

*Oh. Please pardon me, Professor.*

*No offense offered, I'm sure. None taken. And please do not take offense at this, but now is not the time of your life to confront Oedipus. You will remember, and come to him later. The others will not.*

*I'll close now. I've forgotten what I intended when I began to write this letter. Forgetfulness has its reasons, I guess.*

*Errant, but as ever yours,*

*Paul*

\* \* \*

You said before, sir, that Albright was searching for a survivor of the fire, but now you say he is searching for himself?

His self. We're not talking about trying to get properly placed in society.

All right. His self. Or a survivor. Which is it?

I believe every search is a search for the self, but it can't be conducted directly so there's always an intermediary goal—a golden fleece, a woman, a grail. Your search for Albright is a search for your self and the agency's self, though you may think you're only gathering and interpreting data for a particular case. I don't mean to offend.

We don't allow ourselves to be offended.

Very wise.

So who or what is Albright's intermediary?

Someone and maybe also some thing that has survived the fire. He's always known this, but always is not a meaningful way of putting it in the case of Albright.

How would you put it?

Well, for Albright things don't exist in time and space the way they do for you and me. They flare here, there, then, now, like the fireflies in my garden. You have no sense of fireflies flying from place to place. There's just the night dotted with little green fires.

What convinced Albright that someone survived the fire?

I don't know.

Did he come here to ask you about the survivor?

No, he didn't suppose I knew. I think he was just looking for some place to start.

And could you help him?

I had a clue.

Which was?

A number.

The series you left on the phone?

I didn't say it was a series.

We believe it's not a phone number or an address.

I take it you got the number from Ms. Albright.

Only about half the integers. The rest were indecipherable from the data she had. What do you think the number stands for?

I'm afraid my notion of numbers will seem very crude to an adept like you.

I would like to hear it.

Well then, I think numbers are a kind of exudate from a system of symbols like deltas, cross-hatches, inverted arrowheads, that kind of thing, which in turn are a laminate over a self-referential order, which some think approximates the real order of things and some think not.

That's interesting, sir. Where did you get the number?

My gardener found it on a slip of paper tucked under the corner of my doormat.

What else was on the paper?

Nothing.

What made you think of sending it to Albright?

I don't know, but I knew immediately that I would send it to him.

I suppose some might say, sir, that calling a mysterious number to an old friend and leaving no explanatory message would be questionable. Ms. Albright said that her husband is not good with numbers.

That's true. In college he wrote a fine doleful poem about the dark fate of numbers. They were a doomed soldiery marching along the brow of a dusky hill before descending into night. So, under ordinary circumstances I would not send a number to Albright, but the moment I saw the number a powerful intuition told me it pertained to him.

How did he know to come to you? Did he recognize your voice on the phone?

Possibly. But more likely he just wanted to talk to someone from his past. I don't know how he found me. I'm not in the phone book.

You knew him well?

There was no knowing him well. He was unformed.

But he must've thought the two of you had something important in common.

What we had in common was the tutelage of a rare teacher.

Professor John Professor Tyree. He's one of the connections we're investigating. We believe that in his case you might be helpful.

Helpful in what way?

In understanding why he was at the House of Nordquist at the time of the fire.

That may actually be simple. He probably came because Albright was there. He was very fond of him.

We have evidence that the Professor had become mentally unstable.

What evidence?

A letter describing hallucinatory dreams. Did Albright tell you about that?

No. He only told me that Professor Tyree came to the House of Nordquist to be with him. He couldn't persuade him not to. I don't have the evidence you have, but I doubt Professor Tyree was unstable.

Why do you say that?

I would guess that he set himself a course and pursued it to the end. That was his forte as a teacher. He pursued every idea to its logical conclusion. True, he went somewhat mercurially from one idea to another, but in each case he was dogged until he had exhausted the idea's powers of explanation. But now I must break off. I apologize for the abruptness, but I'm tired. This has been interesting but taxing. But by all means stay if you like. We can sit quietly together and enjoy the colors and fragrances of the garden.

Thank you, but I'll be leaving now. May I come again?

Didn't I say you're always welcome? But I warn you I'll keep trying to convince you not to try to enter into Albright's places.

The places that have nothing between, like the fireflies in your garden?

Exactly. Begin by discarding all axioms of your training, all the quid est demonstratum. They will lead you to Albright, but he will be in a place you don't want to enter. If that sounds portentous, so be it.

*　*　*

One particular day I climbed up the hill at daybreak without Deirdre. Remember what it was like up there? Hit or miss garden, weeds, wildflowers. Lots of them bent toward the sun. What's that called?

Heliotropic. But it was more likely just the prevailing west wind.

I like heliotropic better.

The glow of the candle is dimmed by deposits of soot on the interior of the glass chimney.

Deirdre didn't come out, but I heard a knocking on the window of her studio and saw her through the glass though it was dirty and weeded up. She came out. You're early, Alicia. I thought you'd be meeting your sweetheart Paul. We're not sweethearts, I told her. I have a favor to ask. What is that, dear Alicia? I want to meet Helene. She shook her head sadly. That's not possible just now. Why? She's with Eric in his studio. Well I could've said you'd met her, but that wouldn't have done any good, would it?

This is your story.

I was mad. I made my own picture of Helene in my head. Deirdre was leading her off the island. Her hair was black wires. Her face was a white egg, two big black eyes, holes for a nose, and a red slit for a mouth. Can you picture it?

Yes.

Her neck had way more tendons than normal, like they were afraid her head would fall off.

Who's they?

Whoever put her together. Real bony. She didn't have any clothes on, just something flowing down over her like a sheet of dark water. The worst were the hands. Lots of fingers, more than ten. The hands were open like they wanted something to hold. The mouth started to open and close. It made me hold my baby tight.

* * *

*Dear Professor John,*

*I'm grateful for your warnings. Act whenever possible sub species aeternitatis, you told us. Otherwise there would be nothing but the pseudo-values of the marketplace. Sometimes I think everything at the House of Nordquist is under the eyes of eternity. Nothing is mundane.*

*I have to decide between the House of Nordquist and Alice. I don't have much time. It was easy to avoid a decision when I was hauling crates, chipping stone, watching the flashing lights of the synthesizer. Everything was just a fantastical game called Change the World. Then came the peripeteia, the fateful turning you warned us about. But what if the peripeteia occurs without the protagonist recognizing it? Suppose he was sitting with a beloved companion in the forest. Everything was still. They were leaning against a tree, the trunk so solid it might have been the axle of the world. The dome of sky was revolving slowly and evenly around the top of the tree. How could there be a peripeteia in such a world? But there was. The woman Helene came. Outward appearance of utter stillness but inward writhing of pain. A composite pain caused by the hammering of all the nails of our recent history. History. I never did well in history classes. Zeitgeist, thesis and antithesis, teleology. To me it was always just tears and slaughter, hammers and nails. I remember the day Meachem told Professor Aptheker that if history was providential, then God was a sadist. I agreed, but I did not say so. Go and reread the Book of Job, Meachem, the Professor said, and we will talk again. So Meachem and I reread it, aloud. I was Job. He was the comforters. All it did was terrify me a second time. I will never read it again.*

*A stone, a woman every day thinner, serpentine wires, the lights of a machine flashing frantically in search of a pattern, black sarcophagi, a head crowned with fire. This can't be real. I'll wake up and it'll all be gone.*

*Enough. I should have torn this letter up. I promise a different kind next time.*

*As ever,*
*Paul*

* * *

How many more nights you think we can get out of this candle?

The flame, deep in the sooted chimney, flutters in the breath of Alice's speaking.

Three.

Not enough. We have to get to the heart of the fire.

OK.

I never knew a fire could get hot enough to shine through a body so you could see the bones under the flesh.

Probably an illusion.

There were lots of illusions. A house stuck in the ice of the Arctic Ocean, a woman's body with millions of musical sounds in it, a book of pictures of a symphony that will change the world. But what if they weren't illusions? What if the symphony changed the world?

You think it did?

Maybe. But we hardly ever leave the house, so we haven't noticed.

I don't think it did because it never got out into the world.

What if somebody escaped with the symphony in a picture book and now they're out there just waiting for the right moment to play it.

Who would that somebody be?

Maybe Professor Tyree. Maybe he was fire retardant like those pajamas kids wear.

You said we had to get to the heart of the fire.

Maybe the book was at the heart of the fire with the symphony in it and the escapee has it.

Can he play it?

Sure. Right now he's going around playing little snips like seeds on every continent. When he finally plays the whole symphony it won't matter where because the seeds will sprout up and play all over the world.

Ingenious.

The chimney is fixed securely to a brass tripod or it would have fallen when the empty wine bottle tipped over and struck it a glancing blow. The diminishing stub of candle burns near the bottom. The oblique light on the two faces creates the illusion that their brows have been sheared and replaced by chevrons applied with burnt cork.

I can't get it in my head how the symphony in the book is five or six painting.

Why?

Because a symphony could be played in every of corner the world at once, but a painting can be in only one place at the time. Isn't that right?

Pictures can be reproduced thousands of times.

Right. Or you could put the paintings in a movie and play it everywhere. But this is stupid. You want to hear another version?

Yes.

OK. Helene escaped with the book with the idea of getting a big orchestra to play the symphony of her burnt up master and change the world, but an evil agent captured her. He can't figure the book out so he has to torture her until she tells him how to play the book and then he can rule the world. The good guys can't get to him in time to stop him. Only he doesn't get it right and changes the world into a Hell of twisted ruins and fires that never go out. You like that one? I could think up another one. Eric himself is out there with the symphony running from all the agents until he can steal a machine and play it.

You left out a version in which Deirdre is the one that has escaped with the book.

Deirdre doesn't make me think of another version. But what if your body had the right stuff. Eric wouldn't have to send Deirdre to an island to get a half dead immigrant from the holding tank. You could be the one that escaped and is running around with the symphony. Or do you think the body had to be Helene? It had to be you. Nobody else wouldn't do. Remember? Somebody sings it in Casablanca. Never mind. How do you think the movie will end?

I think it's already ended.

No it hasn't.

* * *

Ms. Albright, what if you put aside any effort to get at the bare facts. Concentrate instead on how you imagine it really happened.

That would be fun, but it won't work. Paul and I already tried that. We sat in our kitchen by candlelight. It was very atmospheric like an old movie. The shadows of our heads were doing panto-mimes on the wall, but you couldn't figure out what. We had ghosts outside the window too, blowing around in the wind and whooshing. Once the ceiling disappeared, but nothing came down out of sky except darkness. We drank wine, but a genie didn't come out of the bottle.

OK then let's try something else. Imagine where Paul might be now.

That's an interesting idea. Let's say he's walking down a street, squinting to see the number. Can you picture it?

Yes. In cities house numbers are often hard to see in the dark or are missing.

I didn't say it was a house number. And it's not dark. It's broad daylight, like now, only we don't know it, sitting inside this box with your machine whirring in our ears.

Paul is looking for something.

You don't have to be looking for something to leave home. It could just be a getaway.

But you believe he's looking for something. Imagine what.

You want me just to let it come into my mind without thinking about it?

Exactly.

Right now he's looking up at a window. It's very hot in the City. There's a naked woman up there trying to cool off. A little breeze is flapping a curtain in front of her, so it's not a dirty picture. The woman reminds him of something about the fire. That's because everything reminds him of something about the fire. It's like an ember inside his skull. Wait a minute. A name just came to me.

Tell me the name.

Meachem.

The name is not familiar to you.

Sometime Paul must've said something about him, but it didn't stick. After a while to tell you the truth nothing much that Paul said stuck. The long silences stuck. I thought about running off to meet my older son. Like being in the French Foreign Legion with Gary Cooper. Lots of dangers and thirst. The Rifs and all that. Someday I will.

But you don't know where your older son is.

I could find him. I get picture postcards from all over the world. The last one showed the house where Henrik Ibsen the playwright worked, some kind of lodge pole thing. The logs were so big and furry it looked like a huge animal.

It would be a long trip to Oslo if he's not there.

I wouldn't go to Oslo. You lay out the postcards and connect them in a pattern that tells you where he'll be next. Right now I know he's on his way to the Southwest.

Doesn't sounds like one of his more exotic places.

But it's still dangerous. If you're out around the buttes and misread a smoke signal you could get an arrow in your back.

OK, but right now Paul might be in a more dangerous place than your son.

You mean the City. My son would never go to such a place. There's no sense to being a nomad if you get trapped in a big city.

\* \* \*

Have you seen him again, sir?

Yes.

I'd like to know what took place.

He talked about the lamentable conditions south of here. Run down brownstones, pavements heaved up, curbstones missing. Loiterers. Somebody asked him, whatcha looking for, hoss?

What did he answer?

He didn't know what to answer. He just stood speechless in the middle of the street.

And then what did he do?

You mean where was he next?

All right, where was he next?

He was standing on a doorstep. Across the street on the second floor was an open window, like a frame for a painting. A woman was bathing herself in the fresh morning air. Her hair in the warm wash of early light was the color of a ripening peach, undulant and melodious. The way he described her ignited my senses. We were sitting here in the gazebo, just as you and I are now. I got up and walked out into the garden. The gardener was there. The sun pierced the interstices of his ancient hat and fell on the ground shining like a trove of precious stones.

Quite beautiful, sir.

I meant to emphasize not beauty but the feverish and illusory state of my perceptions, a warning.

The question is how are we to track a person who pops up here and there like the fireflies in your garden?

Track? There's no possibility of tracking. We're talking about places with no ambient space, no time markers, no connections. How did he get into them? Footfalls on the pavement? Ephemeral images half recorded in his eye? A spectral guide moving through urban blight? I have no idea. What's to be said is that you must never enter them. Fortunately you probably can't. But your persistence worries me.

We have no choice but to go into the places where he is.

Then let me try another figure. Albright's past places are nested like Russian dolls—a window, a cloister, a large black book, a frozen ship, the mind of a dwarf, a red demigod. The innermost doll is a fire. I've named only a few. And now present places we know nothing about. We don't know how many, how nested.

I have my assignment.

Tell your superior that the assignment cannot be fulfilled.

If we had to turn away from an assignment, it would certainly not be on grounds of dangerous places.

I thought you would say something like that.

I hope to see you again, sir.

I wish you well. But remember at least this, in Albright's places there must be no you.

* * *

Dear Professor John,

Don't worry that this letter comes before you've had a chance to answer my last two. I'm not going to burden you with questions about the meaning of history. This will be pure description, the thing itself. Meachem would be proud of me. I'll give a title and hold myself to it. Achieve exactness.

### The Wires

The woman Helene approaches a slab of stone. She wears a white robe. The sash is cinched tightly. Rising from the strict margin of the robe the visible flesh is the hue of a shadow on a blanched wall. The stone is a monolith. The story is that two men brought it here from another part of the house. Given its mass, that may seem improbable, but that is the story. The surface of the stone has been inexpertly smoothed. Chisel marks and cuppings mar the surface.

A young man, N, stands to the side, between the stone and one of four large black speakers that stand in the corners of the room. N seems uncomfortable. He appears not to know what to look at, his eyes focused in the middle distance, but sometimes straying to the woman.

A tall red-headed man stands by a large console. A crookneck lamp shines down on the controls. Wires run from a synthesizer to the stone. N rarely looks at the red-headed man.

The woman unties the sash and slips the robe off. There is nothing provocative about her movements. She is emaciated. It is clear to N that she has never been voluptuous, though how he knows this he could not say. She folds the robe neatly into a series of ever smaller triangles, in the manner of a flag to be presented to a war widow. She puts it aside. When the woman lies down on the chill stone, she does not shudder. It may be that her body stiffens against the coldness of the stone, but N can perceive no such rigor. The room is so still that the hum of electricity is clearly audible. The woman arranges the terminals of the wires along the left side of her torso. The terminals look like pucks used in a board game. There are four—red, black, green, and white.

Raven, says the man at the synthesizer. The tone of his voice suggests that the utterance is a signal. N has heard this before and *done some research. Ravens are larger than crows. They are fierce foragers. When they fly, their wings make the sound of a rising wind. Crows' wings are silent. Ravens' eyes are blacker than crows', though technically true black does not admit of degrees. N knows that his research is foolish. The word, as spoken by the tall red-headed man, has nothing to do with birds. It is in fact not a word at all.*

*Raven, says the man at the synthesizer. Something happens in the body of the woman. N feels a trilling in his blood.*

*The operator of the synthesizer begins to adjust the controls of the console. The four speakers produce sound. Perhaps the sound passes at irregular intervals from one to another. N's mind casts about randomly. From a past winter there comes to him the high-pitched sound that coursed back and forth from one end of the beach to the other as the water began to freeze. It sounded to him like the call of some subaqueous creature yearning for its mate. The memory is irrelevant, an errant analogy. In fact at that moment he does not exactly hear anything. Rather he is submerged in a sea of sound. The room is submerged. The house may be submerged. And the hill and the horizon and the sky may be submerged. But he cannot know that.*

*In his body N now feels a long basal vibration that is soon subjected to a series of unsettling alterations— the sudden division of tones into tiny packets, an unmetered pizzicato, the ringing of a bell in air so thin that the relentless attacca of the striking clapper is like an incision of the inner ear. N is disoriented. He knows only that something implacable has taken possession of the room and that it has been created by the red man at the synthesizer transforming the sounds of the body on the stone. A red wash suffuses the entire room, but there is no room.*

*That is the best I can do, Professor John. I can't give you any idea of the duration of this condition. But I can tell you this. Time, which had not seemed to apply in Eric's studio, has breached its walls. It is manifest in the degradation of the woman's body. My mind turns to Professor Aptheker's lecture on The Nativity by de la Tour. He pointed out a sly invasion of crepuscular light. The swaddled baby was already an incipient mummy. There was never a moment in the life of Jesus that was not shadowed by the cross. The same could not be said of the light of the resurrection. Why? I don't remember exactly* what Professor Aptheker said. Something about sin making a light as bright as the resurrection inaccessible to the human eye.

As ever,
Paul

P.S. I was certain that I would dream of the raven, even though I knew the utterance did not signify a bird. It would be flying out of Eric's mouth, enlarging itself as it flew more freely. The one visible eye would be obsidian. The other eye might be red but it would remain invisible because the bird would not turn in its flight. It would fly straight, pulling the walls of the house with it out over the brow of the hill. The Fall of the House of Nordquist. But I did not dream of the raven. I dreamt of the altered sounds of Helene's body. I could not hear them. They were tiny crystalline creatures, dancing in the air like fireflies, visible only when the scant light of the synthesizer's console caught them at certain angles.

This is obviously not a postscript. I'm losing all sense of proportion. I hear Professor Aptheker excoriating modern art's contribution to atheism—moving the deep grounding and perspective of classicism forward until everything becomes a wasteland of shattered planes, broken light, a film of untruth over the eye. I confess, in my mind's eye I see as on the surface of a cracked seashell the obdurate stone, the altar of Eric's will, the shrunken Helene, a bitten wafer, a bloodless wound.

I should tear this non-postscript off, but I won't. Stet.

\* \* \*

Dear Childe Paul,

In your letter of February 25 you prove yourself a true devotee of the ancient dream of stillness, the One in the Many. I must've tried to say this before. I will try to say it again. Think of the cave at Lescaux, the great herds of beasts swarming the walls. No Platonic shadows here. Wild aurochs, horns piercing the sky, great bison *thundering across the stone, huge cullions, stags wearing forests of horns, big bellied mares just before dropping their foals. Fecundity beyond imagining, an explosion of life. But where was the still point, the One? It was not to be found on the walls, though scattered here and there were mysterious little geometries. Was the One inside the white eye of the roasting fire? In the omphalos of the sacred mother, huge-breasted, in the center of dancing circle? In the depthless resonance of chest-pounding and chanting? It had to be there somewhere. Otherwise such massing of life would have maddened humanity in its infancy.*

*Along the bright rim of the moon sing the angelic children of the One. Below, in the hushed chamber of death, the Bishop of Chester bets a trace of fine steeds that Hobbes will recant and call upon the One. But a stroke has rendered the grand old atheist speechless, so the matter can never be adjudicated.*

*Digressions. But apposite. On the one hand your and Alice's unmoving axle tree that holds the bowl of sky to its regular rotation. On the other the disquiet of Eros. Thus are you, as are we all, torn between the wonders of the many and the repose of the One. The ubiquitous human tragedy. Once content in our animal fleshiness, we made the mistake of nourishing consciousness, which we have blamed on the cruelties of evolution. Soon we awarded ourselves a soul. Nominated ourselves creators. Tamed the great herds to paint. O vaunting tragic creature Man.*

*Your letter, though it does not intend to, calls me to your side. I am with you in your deep cave in the House of Nordquist, cave of the winds, cave of forbidden sounds. It is older than the cave of Lescaux. Together we look up at the dark roof of Eric World. We cannot see the fixed stars. We cling to each other. We assure each other that they are there, the Primum Mobile, the impregnable outworks of the universe. For perhaps it is true, as Professor Aptheker might say if he knew the case, that only the Primum Mobile can calm the lights of the machine in their troubled flickering, can teach the woman's body to be as assured as the stone on which it reposes, can quench the fire burning on the head of the towering man, render the four sarcophagi mute.*

*The term ends in six weeks. I am coming to the House of Nordquist. I will knock on the door like an ancient mariner. Surely someone will let me in.*

*In happy anticipation,*
*Professor John*

\* \* \*

I request, sir, that the next time you know he's coming you contact me.

I would be happy to make such a promise, but to what purpose? He comes without announcement, this last time with a purpose you couldn't have made any use of.

Meaning?

Meaning he wanted me to talk about me, not himself.

Talk about you would be very interesting to me, sir. Our research on you is extensive but inconclusive—your achievements at college, your success as a financier and then silence.

Financier is a bit fancy. I was merely an investor.

You must be very adept at numbers.

Successful investing has nothing to do with numbers. Are you familiar with Schrodinger's cat?

Yes.

Then you know that when you open the black box the cat, if an adherent to quantum mechanics, will be both dead and alive. If the cat is Newtonian he will prefer one state or the other. To be a successful investor you bet always on the quantum cat. The occasional cat that is only dead is just part of the cost of doing business.

Our research shows that there was a great stir to discover your equations.

Yes, but there were no equations. Econometrics. A scam that pretends you can assign numbers to the behavior of billions of people because en masse they are predictable—wars, revolutions and the like being unimportant. Not to speak of the antics of the natu-

ral world. But we have gone astray. Albright was not interested in
my life as an investor.

What was he interested in?

He wanted to know when the peripeteia of my life came.

I'm not familiar with the term.

A fateful turn of events. In his case the arrival of the woman Helene at the House of Nordquist. But it was my peripeteia he
wanted to hear about.

I would also be interested to hear about it.

All right. My peripeteia was the arrival of a voice that said you
must renounce your identity.

Renounce your identity?

Yes, I had an identity of crystal clarity. I was of all of Professor
Tyree's students the one of clearest purpose. So I became successful
and rich, briefly a luminary among the alumni of Justin and James,
until I disappeared from the world of finance. But even during my
days as a shining student and later as a star capitalist Professor
Tyree never loved me as he loved Albright.

Why?

Because secretly he loathed clarity. What he loved was the
shadowy aura that hovers around the edges of clarity. It was there,
he believed, that the verities were to be found. But in class I insisted
on sheering away the aura and leaving only naked clarity. I would
have made a splendid recruit for your agency.

No doubt. What you say about Professor Tyree is paradoxical,
but it makes sense.

I speculate that if you're a grotesque you will not easily rec-
oncile yourself to a world of lucidity. Anyway, as a student, and for
a number of years after, I felt compelled to be clear, or the Nemos
of the world would suck me into their maelstrom of obscurantism.

How did Professor Tyree get the name of Nemo?

I don't know. It's possible it was given to him by Professor
Aptheker. Or he might have given it to himself. Anyway, it fit. Improbable dwarf. Intellectual shape-shifter. Lover of words, because
he knew how slippery words are. He wooed Albright with words.
If he'd had a different body he might've offered himself to Albright
as a lover.

We can come back to that, but you were saying that there came a time when you knew you had to divest yourself of clarity. What led you to that?

Clarity had become a prison. Clarity is indispensable for making large sums of money, but it's reductive. Nemo understood that. I give him credit. One looks in the mirror and sees always the same flat image. One wants to find something utterly surprising. This will seem incongruous to one like you who must always aim at clarity.

True. But go on. Did you divest yourself of clarity?

Yes.

How?

First I had to find a deconstructive place. There are many places nowadays, of course, where radical decentering has led to colorful episodes of rapine, genocide and assorted methods of carnage, but I was not interested in blood. I chose to go up the Amazon, where I believed the sanguineous conquests of the colonialists had settled into humdrum oppression. I landed in Manaus. Nothing there is stable—race, language, history, black river, brown river. Every day erases the day before, and no tomorrow has a hook on which to hang hope. You're nodding. Have you been to Manaus?

No, but we've followed men into places such as you describe. They unravel.

Unravel. That's interesting. My mind jumps across a large field populous with propositions to this one: my gardener wouldn't unravel no matter where he was.

That's an odd proposition.

Why? I told you he's an archetype. He might register a certain foreignness, but he's elemental. He would be unaffected by the inhabitants. Nothing would happen to him. But I was not elemental. I had a burdensome clarity. I had become the most prosaic of men. So I determined to change utterly. So I went to Manaus.

And did what?

Donned a perverse costume, walked the streets of Manaus in a white linen suit and a straw hat accented by a band of yellow silk. Replica of a colonial grandee. Radical displacement. I was sure I would be assaulted by ridicule, opprobrium, broken into pieces, a despised anachronism.

You're looking at me strangely.

Yes. I apologize. For some reason I'm thinking that Albright may have looked like you once, his youthful face burnished with the desire to understand, in his case one he may have taken to be a demigod.

We were in Manaus.

Right. The disguise of a colonial grandee didn't work. People didn't see me. They walked through me. I was permeable, invisible. You may be thinking that might have sufficed. But erasure wasn't what I was after. I wanted to be broken into pieces that I could put back together any way I chose.

So what did you do?

I took the opposite tact. I threw off my faux colonial splendor and plunged into the motley masses there wearing rags. People shouted at me in various languages. Pinched their noses. Poofed and waved me away. A stinking beggar. Worse than a mestizo, an animal. Some even struck me. Vulgarians ripped away my rags and held out my genitalia for ridicule. They pulled my hair out in tufts. I willingly, even enthusiastically, played the part of a thing despised, but I was still not sufficiently broken. I built a hovel of sticks by the bank of the river. A crowd of lawless youths tore it apart. They smeared my own feces on me. I broke down. I babbled in unknown tongues, howled like an animal, crawled along the bank like a furtive saurian. I crammed reeds and mud into my mouth. Success at last. I was broken.

You suffered terribly.

I visited it all upon myself.

How did you manage to come back?

I never came back. That was the whole point.

You say you told this story to Albright.

Yes.

How did he receive it?

It's hard to tell how he receives anything, but I think he understood.

He didn't say anything?

He nodded.

You will call us when he returns. I trust you.

Really?

Yes. I know from the way you tell your story.

Interesting. Albright and I once had a teacher who held that nothing could engender faith so powerfully as a story, and that there was one story so compelling that it was inescapable.

Did you escape it?

Nominally, but once you've heard it you can never escape it completely. It came back to me when I was an animal foraging on the bank of the Negro. It whispered insistently that there was nothing I could do to forfeit my immortal soul. At the time I hated it for saying that.

Do you still?

No.

Did Albright escape it?

No, but he doesn't know it. He never went to Manaus. He doesn't understand what perfect clarity of purpose does to those who enter its domain. Neither do you.

* * *

Did I tell you about seeing Helene sitting next to Deirdre on the divan?

You said you imagined her because Deirdre wouldn't let you see her.

The room was made of diagonal stripes, remember? The light was focused through the window in two rays, one for each woman.

Alice laughs dryly. The twin images of candle flame in the chimney and in the window dance with a momentary jollity.

I remember most the hands. Did I already tell you this?

Go on.

She was holding her hands out like a beggar. No, not like a beggar. More gentle. I would've liked to put something in her hands, like a bluebird's egg, something small and pretty, but that's not what she wanted. She wanted something to eat. It scared me. I held my baby tight. I already told you this, didn't I?

Go on.

It wouldn't have done any good if I'd had something for her to eat.

Why?

Because as fast as she got something to eat, she had to lie on the stone and give it up. Right?

Yes.

I didn't know what to do. Maybe I should've run around the house screaming bloody murder and hollering that Eric was killing her. Cassandra, right?

Yes.

I didn't holler. I played being Alicia. I went to the window and lay in the grass and looked into Deirdre's studio. Deirdre was painting in the black book. I saw it. It looked like tiny creatures crouching under something like a boat turned upside down without any skin on its ribs. Everything was whited out, the sky and the ground. I don't know what the creatures were doing, nothing maybe, just freezing to death. Deirdre looked up and saw Alicia looking in the window. Alicia didn't run away. She remembered that one time Deirdre said if she painted Alicia, she would love to paint the wildness of her hair. Which is hard because there are over one hundred thousand hairs on the human head. Did you know that?

You said you never saw the paintings in the book.

I lied to you, but it was a kindly lie. I didn't want you to feel left out. What do you guess a painting of my wild hair would've looked like?

I don't know. I never saw any of those later paintings.

Right. Stick to your story.

* * *

We're in contact with a person who's been talking to Paul in the City.

Who?

An old classmate.

Meachem?

Yes. He may be important in the search for Paul. Have you remembered any more about him since his name came to you?

I never saw him, but for some reason I can imagine him, very distinguished and suave, sleek black hair that will never turn gray no matter how old he gets, like he's sold his soul to the Devil. Rich. He's probably in Who's Who in America.

He told our agent Paul was in search of his self.

That would be tough, finding something you never totally had.

It's hard to imagine a person without a self.

I know, but Paul was a living eraser. He erased everything until there was just a pile of little black eraser worms on his desk. Not even the best crime lab could scrape them up and figure out what was erased.

A striking metaphor, Ms. Albright.

One time I almost let myself get erased. It would've been a willing act. I was going to get transferred into a picture. There wouldn't be any name under it. I would be boiled down to just the hairs of my head. No other features. I wouldn't have been recognizable, even if I was in the black book and was saved from the fire.

I believe we will soon have the book and the one who escaped from the fire. Meachem said that for Paul to complete his search he had to find a certain person. He didn't say who. But I bet you have a good idea.

It would have to be a totally changed person. Which reminds me of a story Paul told me about a woman who got changed into a tree. Do you know about Paul's and my trees?

Yes, they were in the letters.

That's right. I forgot. Well one day I walked around the trees three times. I cast a spell. I thought it worked. Paul and I got married. But I didn't know at the time that he would erase everything we did together.

\* \* \*

Dear Professor John,

Though I long to see you, I can't encourage you to come here. The House of Nordquist has now completely turned in on itself. The moment Helene entered, the doors shut. I'm the only outsider who has a key, the prison's only trustee. Every day the gap between the house and the world grows wider. I have to leap farther and farther. Someday I'll miss and plunge into the void. Or to change the metaphor, think of me as the last mooring line. Once I'm cast off, the House of Nordquist will sail away on the wind of Eric's symphony, land in a New World and establish the Novum Ordo Seclorum.

Everything will be changed, but only for a while. The old cycle will begin again. Rise and Fall. The world clotted again with uninterpretable events, like a fatal thickening of blood. Then in despair we'll have to designate another Eric. Every age exuding its own fatal precipitate.

Strange thoughts. I told you I never understood history.

Faithfully I keep my rendezvous at the House of Nordquist, the witness. I had my moment on the stone. My body did not resonate. But my flesh had intimations. I felt the stone's hunger. I ought to have been glad that Eric rejected me, but I wasn't. On the stone I felt a trilling in the blood. I yearned to give myself up, the chosen one. I saw the dancing lights of the machine. I heard the brumble of the speakers, the transformed sound of my breathing. But in the end my body didn't emanate enough history. It hadn't suffered enough. It couldn't reverberate with a whole century of war and blood. The body would have to be Helene. Eric knew she was out there somewhere and his mother would find her for him.

I never saw Eric as a boy. What if I'd been at the cottage a dozen years ago and looked up to at the hill? Here's what I imagine. Eric behind a crude wooden sled he'd made from the broken timbers of the frozen ship, whip in hand, driving the dogs across the ice, southward, the brown hope of tundra just beginning to shimmer in the distance. Never looking right or left, always lashing the dogs with the whip. The dogs' coats bloody, the fur of his mantel and the earflaps of his ushanka swept backwards in the frigid wind. On and on, never swerving, knowing that one day, never mind how many years later, he would arrive in the studio, would find a naïve helper to assist him with the installation of stone, speakers, synthesizer, to stand near the instruments and witness the extraction of history from the most memorious body in the land.

It is a terror to be in the presence of one who never swerves, who never makes a random motion of any kind, who never speaks because words are clotted with approximation. And Helene. I can't bear to look at her anymore though I'm the consecrated witness. Someday her body will have surrendered all its music. It will disintegrate. Her flesh will all be consumed, nothing but white bones on grey stone and even they slowly turning to dust. Can these bones live, Professor Aptheker? No.

Fortunately for you I have to close. Hardware time. Washers and nuts and bolts slip mischievously from one bin to another. Nails tumble from their bins and clatter on the floor. Rakes lose their balance and topple from their racks into the aisle. Stud-finders spin without proximity of ferrous metal, plumb lines send into the air a haze of blue chalk.

Dear Professor John, I urge you not to come here. The place and the time are out of joint.

As ever,
Paul

\* \* \*

We're going to give the story a name. "The Lost Air."

Very romantic.

Right. A ghost woman in black walking along a high cliff, a swirling river, and all that. But it'll be hard to work in the investigator.

You don't have to work him in. He hasn't happened yet.

Yes, but I'm Cassandra, right? I know what's coming. Besides, he's already called on the telephone. Telephone calls have to be worked in even if what's said hasn't happened yet.

You haven't told me what he said.

He was very polite. He said he'd get back to us to ask for a meeting later. But you're right. We'll wait and work him in when he happens. Right now the story is about Deirdre finding Helene. The investigator is just foreshadowed, right?

Or fantasized.

Wrong. This guy is real. Nobody would phone and pretend he was an investigator unless it was a scam artist asking for your social security or account number. But we're not to him yet. We're to Deirdre. You can't just skip down to any part of the story you want.

OK.

At the time of this story, remember, there was this thing that Deirdre was hiding near her body. It was like a mirror but you couldn't see anything in it. So, to figure it all out Alicia had to listen carefully to everything Deirdre said in case she made a slip and gave away an important clue about what was going on.

I think you'd already figured it out.

That's the Cassandra thing, which is very hard to get into the story, somebody nobody ever listens to.

Then leave her out for now.

The island Deirdre went to, to pick Helene out, was a place for immigrants in quarantine.

Helene had a disease?

She had the disease of history. Just like you told me. You don't remember that?

No.

I need for you to remember the important stuff. Otherwise I have to keep repeating the set-up and the story gets boring. What do you call that?

Exposition.

I thought those were fairs, but never mind. Deirdre picked Helene out from a bunch of women. Can you guess how she picked her out?

No.

She listened. The matron of the quarantine didn't know what was going on. She thought Deirdre was a nun and let her walk down the aisles. Deirdre had to listen very carefully because what if she made the wrong pick? Or maybe there never could've been a wrong pick. Do you believe in fate?

No.

One time you said characters want to be in a different story. But they don't have any choice, right?

Not a choice of stories, but a choice of actions.

Then they can change the story.

I guess you could say that.

I don't want to say it. Helene had to be in Eric's story whether she wanted to or not. Deirdre didn't have to explain to Helene about Eric and the House of Nordquist. She just had to pick her out and take her back. Right? But what if Helene had said she wouldn't come?

I guess that could have happened.

Which shows that something that's bound to happen just barely happens instead of something else. Why do you think Helene came?

I don't know.

Maybe she just wanted to get it over with. Lie down on the stone and give it all up. What do you think?

I never could tell what Helene was thinking.

We don't know much of anything, do we? What are we going to tell the investigator?

We don't have anything new to tell him that we didn't tell the first investigators.

You can tell him about the phone call you got yesterday. Who was it from?

I don't know. The person just left a number.

But I bet you recognized the voice unless he had a handkerchief over the mouthpiece.

I think it was an old college friend.

I never went to college. Do you think I would've known what to do if I had?

What to do about what?

What was going on. Would it have said in some book or lecture what to do when you are Cassandra?

No.

\* \* \*

*Dear Professor John,*

*This is oblique, but it still probably transgresses propriety. Alice was waiting for me as I came out of the back door of the hardware. She knew I was due at the House of Nordquist. She led me to our place in the trees, making it a kind of detective game. Here's how we'll do it. We'll go to the end of Market Street and head north up the hill. A weird house that looks like a ship will come into view. We'll circle around it and go down into the woods.*

*I played along. You sure we won't be seen?*

*Yes. Just follow me.*

*I walked behind her. It was strange. It was as if I'd never seen her before. A middling pretty girl with a shock of brown hair frizzled and wispy around the edges so that the dusky light shone through. A lithe body in a loosely fitting white dress, short, without much waist. Legs sinewy behind the knees, the muscular calves of a hill person. This is Alice, I had to remind myself.*

*Soon we crested the hill and began our descent along the west flank. The fragrance of scattered evergreens rose up to meet us.*

*I know that the sight of my body caused her pain. Pale, almost hairless. I know she felt a welling of pity. I could see it in her eyes. Maybe all nakedness is pitiable. Maybe all women know, practically from birth, that a man's nakedness is pitiable, a useless corpus of flesh unless he's inflamed. How generous she was. No thought of the pain to come. Her gaze fearless. The trees receded. The hill surrendered its pitch. I started to write that at that moment she surely won a victory over Eric. That would have been a shallow thing to say. Her motives were obviously deeper, so much deeper that I don't want to sully them with obtuse guesswork.*

*I'm sorry to have inflicted this on you. But I had to write it. If it had remained hidden it would have come between us. I do not want that.*

As ever,
Paul

\* \* \*

We know that we're close to him now, sir. It would be a great help if we had the number you were given.

It wouldn't do you any good. Whatever the number is, he's in a different place now. And, as I keep saying, you can't be there.

If we believed that we would have to hypothesize that there exist inaccessible places.

And who knows what might exist in such a place. The missing book of paintings by Deirdre Nordquist, it therefore also inaccessible.

I would like to suggest, sir, that this talk of inaccessible places is not furthering the investigation.

I understand your frustration. It is hard for you to contemplate something that has no context, is not contingent, is not a compound, something so pure that it requires abstinence. But if the database is to be complete, there can be nothing forbidden, right?

We're not a nunnery.

Noli me tangere Albright's old religion professor would warn you. In Albright's case not untouchable divinity, but something just as imperative.

Can you say that another way?

I will try. Think of a picture. In the foreground is a pleasant lawn, in the middle ground a reverend old house with white pillars, in the background green hills. The kind of image one might see in a commercial calendar. But suppose there was no ground at all. I mean the sure everyday sense we have that there is a solidity on which everything stands. It may be invisible. But it is there, a guaranty of our standing and our stepping. Now take that ground away and you have some idea of Albright's places.

It makes me think of a holograph floating in space. Is that what you mean?

Close. But a holograph is just a trompe l'oeil. Albright's places are really groundless.

Why doesn't Albright himself disappear in them?

I don't know. He has some special dispensation. You don't have it.

But you must have it if you can safely sit here with him.

I don't know how safely, but yes for now I appear to have it. I don't know why. And I fear it's provisional. Every time Albright appears on my front steps, I don't know if house and garden will disappear.

With all due respect, sir. I think that's not rational. Nature hates a void.

It's your agency that hates a void. Most of nature is a void. We live on a little island.

* * *

I'm afraid this will sound cruel, Ms. Albright, but we're convinced Paul will not come back on his own. We have to find him and bring him back.

Why cruel? You've pretty much said that all along. On his own what would he come back to?

To you. To the scene of the fire.

I forgot about the scene of the fire. In the movies the criminal always comes back to the scene of the crime. So you can stakeout some agents and nab him when he shows up.

We haven't said it's a crime scene.

The other agent said the fire started in Eric's studio and was not an accident.

Yes, that's the current hypothesis.

Paul had a religion professor who taught that every story is a crime story. Cain and Abel. It never ends.

That may be theologically sound, but in the world of law not every story is a crime story. Anyway I'm happy to report that the odds of our finding Paul are now very good.

Paul doesn't believe in odds.

He doesn't have to believe in them. If enough traces are found, the probability of a sighting mounts until it's a virtual certainty.

And if you find him you think he'll be able to tell you who started the fire and who escaped?

That's one reason we're talking to you, to get insights that will help us persuade Paul to tell us what he knows.

A wife can't be made to testify against her husband.

We're not talking about testimony, Ms. Albright, just help in arriving at the facts.

I wonder if you'll ever have all the facts.

We still have much work to do.

If you want my opinion, it was a crime of passion.

\* \* \*

In the window the barren branches of the ash, like the fingers of empty hands, open on two candlelit faces.

You talk for once.

What do I look like in the candlelight?

You look like a pirate.

You look like a sibyl.

I thought sibyls hung upside down.

That was a special case. Most were prophets, like you.

Did I prophesy a fire?

You prophesized that the great musical work would end in disaster.

Nobody listened.

Not your fault.

This is old stuff. There's something else on your mind.

I have to make a trip.

You never make trips.

I got a call I have to answer.

Where are you going?

Down to the City.

Where in the City?

All I have is a number.

You're not a numbers person.

Why do you say that?

Numbers people know how to add things up.

What didn't I add up?

You didn't add up Eric and the stone and the machine and all that, or you would have known the odds against him were impossible.

I added you up.

I was easy, a small town uneducated girl.

That isn't what I meant.

There is an islet of silence. The flame of the candle steadies itself.

You also didn't add up the odds against your beloved Professor Tyree.

I wrote him not to come.

Maybe. Where are the letters you wrote him anyway?

They're in my desk. Deirdre gave them to me. She got them from Professor Tyree when he came to the house. You can read them if you want.

I know that's the story. When the agent comes, he'll want to see them.

So, give them to him.

I bet they're scorched.

I didn't notice. Deirdre had them tied up with blue ribbon. I didn't read them for a long time.

When you did, what did you find out?

They were pretty much what I remembered—falling in love with you, getting hooked on Eric.

Why didn't Professor Tyree give them to you himself when he came?

We've been over this.

Tell me again. I love weird stories.

I never saw him. Deirdre made a room ready for him. She brought me the letters. She said he wanted me to read the last one, which I hadn't read yet, and then we would meet the next day. But then there was the fire.

What was so special about the last letter?

You need to read it for yourself.

OK. So you're going on a trip. I know it's important for you not to tell me what you're going to do in the City, like hiding the letters all these years.

I didn't hide them.

I wish I hadn't mentioned them. They make me remember my lost son. If I read the letters will they make me remember that Professor Tyree loved you? Don't bother to answer. He was bound to come. I actually thought maybe he could get you free of Eric. But you forgot to tell me how ugly he was, so you can imagine the shock when he limped up on our porch and knocked on the door.

I didn't know how to tell you.

OK, I was worried about Eric, not the Professor. In fact I imagined your relationship with the Professor had a kind of oddball beauty to it, a Greek thing. Anyway maybe I thought somebody that ugly and with all those words would have powers and could get us free of the House of Nordquist. No, I didn't really think that. I always knew he would be a flop. The Cassandra thing.

I wasn't thinking about his powers. I was going to tell him to go back home.

What about you? Are you going to come back home?

Yes.

What do you think you're going to find on this trip?

Black box.

It's Eric, isn't it? Listen. If Eric was still out there, we'd know it, wouldn't we?

Somebody would know it.

And you're going to the one who knows, right? Because you've got his number.


* * *


*Dear Childe Paul,*

*Once you wrote of a veil across the portico of your mind. Within it the scene of Eric on the beach appears. And now another veil, Eric's music. Eye and ear veiled. But the fragrant touch of Alice escapes the veils. How privileged I am that you allow me a glimpse into these most intimate moments of your life. In my mind's eye the treetops of your sacred copse spread their arms over the two of you like the wings of an angel.*

*But to return to Eric. Let's say you are determined to free yourself from the veils. It will be much easier to escape the beach than to escape the music. Music is deeper than image. It's in the old serpent brain, just east of Eden. But, you're wise enough to know that erasure and muting are not really the course. I leave it to you, the poet, to construct an expressive metaphor. My pedant's mind drifts into clichés—waded in too deep, point of no return, etc. I used to advise you to get away from Eric. Now I say stay your course. If you fled now, your mind would become a palimpsest underwritten by ineradicable images and sounds, the black sarcophagi drumming away all hope of forgetfulness. So it's steady on now, Childe Paul. What had been entirely another's story is now also yours.*

*As often happens these days, especially when I'm writing, Aptheker appears. In God's creation, he assures me, there are no pentimenti. On this occasion he is speaking of the pentimento in Caravaggio's* The Taking of Christ. *The arm of Judas is shortened because the artist had planned the spaces of canvas inadequately. And if that were not enough, the artist has painted himself into the scene. And you know how Aptheker hates the self-referential. A special disease of our time already foreshadowed by the wicked Italian. There are no vulgarizations of the sacred beyond the deviance of*

*Caravaggio's brush. Aptheker dares me to dispute the case. I don't want to. The betrayal in the garden, the sleepy disciples, the denials of Peter—these are the very parts of the story that doubt cannot taint because for a few moments the awesome narrative is entirely within our human reach. But bring the Christ back on stage and we are once more in the presence of the numinous, out of our depth. Anyway our dour theologian is right. The Caravaggio is a corruption. Glinting steel, histrionic alarm, a mysterious stigma over Jesus' brow where no crown of thorns has yet been placed, Christ's fingers latticed instead of open to receive the bitter cup.*

*I've wandered. I want to finish by saying that I understand I can never be a pillar, nothing like Alice's support, love unsullied by wordiness and deformity. My only claim to usefulness comes from your letters, which have made me a partner, however unworthy, in your trials. And I must confess that Eric and his project challenge me. Here is a man utterly detached from the mundane. If I can help you plumb the mystery, I offer my life. If that seems to you excessive, strike it. But I will come with all that I have.*

*Yours in anticipation,*
*John*

*P.S. The other day I received a card from Meachem. From Wittenberg(sic). He declares himself a wanderer and a perpetual doubter. Maybe. But not for long. That fiercely centered ego requires a fixed pole and purpose. Mark me.*

* * *

I wasn't sure I'd ever see you again.
We got close to him, sir.
We?
Yes. Three of us. I as coordinator, a back-up, and an analyst.
Three.
Yes, the combination always works.

There's no such thing as always. And three is an ill-advised number.

Why do you say that?

It's agglutinated with myth. And Albright has a dangerous affinity for myth.

We found his fingerprints in an old one-story house.

It wasn't one-story. The stairwell has been blanked off behind a cloak closet.

Stop playing with me.

What did you encounter in the house?

An old woman reported he'd been there. Why are you smiling? I thought you wanted to help.

I do. What did the old woman say?

She described a man in his sixties, which is not surprising because we have evidence that he is prematurely aged. You've seen him. Would you say so?

I would agree. What else did she say?

She said he came with a piece of paper in his hand with a number on it.

How did she sound when she spoke? Was her voice steady or did it quaver?

It was steady. I know what you're thinking. No, it was not Deirdre Nordquist, escaped from the fire. This old woman did not wear a long robe. She did not glide.

Did she seem possessed by an insatiable hunger?

No. It was not the woman Helene, escaped from the fire. She did not speak with an accent.

Did she say anything about the black book?

No. Do you have any idea who she is?

Yes, she is an archetype. Do you know how many before you have seen this old woman?

That's a strange question.

Do you know how many have dreamed her?

Even stranger.

Some dreamers in the throes of their dream of her can't move. They have forgotten the word that will release them. Some keep meeting her at the door over and over. They can't make the dream go any further. Some forget where the door was and wander the streets forever in search of her. Some enter and mount the stairway you didn't see and wind their way upward until they lose sight of themselves.

This is all like a dream, sir. Not worthy of you.

You should advise your superiors to revise their protocols so that you can take seriously the truth of dreams.

Dreams are a fact, but there is rarely any truth in them.

All right, but I can tell you it won't do any good to go back to the house. You would find it changed. The old woman would be gone.

We weren't planning on going back. We have to find Albright's next place. It can't be too far away. We'll find him.

I'm going to give you the number that came to me on a scrap of paper, because you believe it's an important fact. But remember, numbers may not have referents. They can be null, or a trap.

* * *

Well, have your men in the City found him?

We're close. But back to the fire, Ms. Albright. You said you thought it was a crime of passion.

If you watch movies you'll know a crime of passion doesn't have to be a bloody act somebody does when they're out of their head. The prosecution will show that the defendant's passionate hatred of the deceased crystallized into cold calculated murder.

Yes, but we also know there was a lot of electrical equipment in the studio, and faulty wiring can often cause a fire.

I like talking to you but you're being tricky. You already said the fire wasn't an accident.

We're always testing and retesting hypotheses.

Well I can tell you that the accident hypothesis is a bad one. E (I've decided never to say that name again) didn't do any faulty wiring or anything else faulty. Everything was exactly what he willed. Even down to where everybody was looking.

I suspect you mean what Paul looked at.

Yes. E willed Paul to look at certain things, like dials and screens. He wasn't supposed to look at Helene's body, but he didn't want to anyway because it was beginning to make him sick.

Yes, her emaciation is vividly described in the letters.

The electric things that got stuck to Helene left suction marks, like leeches. Paul could see the blood rising under the skin. What if the blood started to escape? Who could look at that?

Nobody unless they were forced to.

In the vampire movies when Bela Lugosi's teeth got near the woman's beautiful neck I hid my eyes.

Helene's neck, according to the letters, was not beautiful.

No, it was all strung together with tendons like a doll before they put the skin on. In the movies the blood was a trick. It squirted out of the fake teeth. With Helene it would be real. Anyway, if Paul ever did look at the neck, E got down on him because he was supposed to be watching the dials.

I thought Eric didn't say anything by that time.

He didn't. He signaled Paul with his eyes. All he ever said was raven, not the bird.

The setting of the dials must've been very critical.

Maybe, but the main thing was that if people aren't looking in the right direction, it changes everything in the room.

I think that idea has been discredited, Ms. Albright, that the observer's gaze can affect what he's looking at, if the thing is inanimate.

It would happen in our kitchen that Paul would look away just when I said something I thought he would have to answer, and my words would go out the window.

He understood the power of your words.

It's true words can have power, especially names. When E named Paul No-Name it made Paul smaller and weaker. When Deirdre named me Alicia she thought I would see things her way. And sometimes I let myself see things her way, but most of the time I saw things my way. I could even see, from what Paul described for me, the sounds of Helene's body going up and down on the green screen. And the red and green and white lights dancing around. I could see Paul look away from the dial when he wasn't supposed to and the green waves knot up like ratted hair and E would stare him down and say raven.

You have extraordinary powers, Ms. Albright.

I didn't have the power to see how Deirdre kept Helene alive. E had all the power.

But the fire stopped him.

I don't think Paul believes that. To him E is still out there somewhere, in this world or another one, with the black book waiting to play the symphony. It's like holding your breath for twenty years. And now he's breathing again, off on a trip. Who could've guessed?

* * *

*Dear Childe Paul,*

*I fear this will seem a strange letter. But don't be worried. We will sort out all things when I come to you, hardly a week away now. Last night I had a suppositional dream. That is, upon waking I either remembered it, as one ordinarily remembers a dream, or I extracted it from a present emotion and inserted it into memory. How can we distinguish between what is truly dreamed and what some mental errancy injects? In the dream, or whatever it was, I was in the Cave of Chauvet. I had no trouble entering. The guards have become lax. To them I was just a clump of saxifrage worried by the wind that constantly blows along the sheer face of the surrounding stone. And of course I knew the code for the electronic number pad that unlocks the steel door. I can't remember it now, but it was long, longer than a phone number. The intention of my dream led me directly down the metal walkway to the interior chamber where the huge bison is, the one with eight legs, the ancient artist's way of indicating the rhythmic running of the beast. I heard the variously pitched drumbeat of* hooves. *So here, I thought, is the first octave, long before Pythagoras, resounding in the breasts of the earliest members of our species. All around the cave roamed the Neanderthals with their thick skulls and strong arms. But they knew not harmony.*

*The next day. I have had another dream, more proximate and more disturbing. Also suppositional, its details clearly derived from your reports. I find myself in a room deep in the House of Nordquist. You, I know, are close by, but I cannot get to you. This is strange. The walls are not impermeable. I am not a prisoner. I think, all right I don't have to come to you in Eric's studio. I will simply walk down the hill to your cottage, gravity that old Devil a friend for once. I will wait for you there, perhaps in the blessed company of your beautiful Alice. But I don't move. It has nothing to do with physical restraint. It has to do with time. The time is not ripe. Or as Aptheker would say, it is not the acceptable time. So, a temporary barrier of time. Temporary, time. Who but Nemo could couple those words in a single sentence, even in the report of a dream? Nemo, father of paradox, the only fathering nature has allowed him. So I give you my child, my dream paradox: all in the House of Nordquist is permeable except for the one barrier of time. Wait, the barrier says. Wait for the acceptable time. But all that is only in a dream, dear Childe Paul. I will come within the week and the barrier will fall.*

*But there was more to the dream. Eric appeared. At first he seemed radically different from your descriptions of him. Keep in mind that unlike your first sighting of him, I had no rich mise-en-scène—sunny beach, vernal river sloughing off its winter skin, mystic mother, joyous chorus of children. I had only the man himself. Eric in the hatchway of my dream. I thought, is this Paul's world-changer? This shabby warlock with sickly pallorous flesh? Unkempt red hair and hawk nose do not a Weltumformer make. But in a matter of moments he was utterly changed, as if a transfiguring wash had flowed over the original tatterdemalion and left in its place a shining demigod, the Fire-bringer, bearer of the Novus Ordo Seclorum. Was this, in the heart of dream, the anteriority of Aptheker, in whose theology a disfigured and despised creature is displaced by a being of blinding radiance? In any case, some power, I cannot say what, had erased all contingencies of clothing, hair, skin and brought forward the creature himself. Ecce Homo.*

*Don't worry, Childe Paul. Allow this exorbitance for now. The passage of time will correct it. Meanwhile we consent to the logic of dream. Did Eric speak, the man of acid silence? Yes. You know what. Raven. The word came so purely into my hearing that I thought it borne not upon the air, but rather ignited in the auricles of my ear. And then the hatchway was empty.*

*I repeat, don't worry, Childe Paul. I will come. There will be clarity.*

*Yours ever closer to the day,*

*Professor John*

\* \* \*

I've come to tell you, sir, that the number you gave me was not a street address.

I never said it was.

It was geological coordinates in disguise.

I doubt it. Numbers don't disguise themselves. But never mind. What did you find at the coordinates?

A locus in the Atlantic Ocean not far from the North Pole.

Was there a ship there?

This was just a locus indicated by numbers. There was nothing in it.

There's no such thing as a place with nothing in it. It would not be a place. It would be hypothetical and dangerous.

You are referring to Albright's places, which you have never explained adequately, though I know you have tried.

Right. They are not empty, but they have attributes that make them uninhabitable.

Like what?

Intensity, concentration, centrifugal force.

You mean like a maelstrom?

Yes, something like that.

But you inhabit them.

Briefly, and every moment I'm shaken by fear.

Why did the number put us in the Arctic? Is Albright there again in his imagination with Eric Nordquist?

No. The Arctic is not imaginary. It's real. It's not a dreamland where a mad old man could fall over the edge into absolute zero. You and your men could visit it with impunity if you were properly equipped. You could witness the vast unending ice, be buffeted by howling winds and come back alive.

Our job is to go where Albright is, not where he's not. The number was a red herring.

So it seems.

My instructions are to post a watch nearby to alert me when Albright comes again since you never know when it will be

Your watch won't see him entering. Worse, he may wander into one of the uninhabitable places we've been talking about.

We have to take our chances, sir.

* * *

*Dear Husband Paul,*

*This shows that anybody can write a letter, not just college boys. Not that it will be like those highfalutin letters you and Professor Tyree wrote. And when I finish this one I'm going to write a letter to my younger son. I know. I don't have an address. So what? I'm going to ask him if he saved the black book. Do you think anybody could really paint music so you could play it again?*

*Writing a letter is fun. You can put down anything you want and imagine the other person's face when they read it. I can see why you and the Professor got into it.*

*I don't think you're going to find the one you're looking for down there in the City. You know why? Maybe he didn't burn up, but once he left that house he would be just another person on the street. Never mind the long red hair. People don't pay much attention to anything like that anymore, especially now that kids have spiked green hair and rings growing out of their lips.*

*Back to the music and whether anybody could play the paintings, I mean if you had a machine like E's. One day Deirdre told me how she was doing the paintings. She imagined a mirror reflecting colors glowing with sounds. I bet that was the thing she was hiding I never could quite see. She said she held the shape she painted close to her breast until she needed it, like a baby. Maybe that was because she just barely missed being barren. E was her only child and already the father was old.*

*The investigator keeps after me about who started the fire. E started the fire. I know that. Only I don't know whose hands he put the match in. Maybe his own.*

*I'm trying to figure out how to get this letter to you. I'm not worried about it being incriminating. I'll probably just leave it on your desk where you can find it. The investigators will read it, but it won't do them any good. They'll put it back. Check out the signature. I'll bet it's the first time you've ever seen it.*

*Your loving wife,*
*Alice*

* * *

Yes, Albright came again. But your watch didn't see him, right?

Yes.

Ah. I see it in your face. The watch disappeared. He probably came into the house despite your orders to the contrary.

Not to the contrary.

Then his disappearance is on your conscience. And you'll have to answer to your superiors.

It was my superiors who ordered the entry.

Even worse.

Did you see the agent come in?

No. He might've been skulking behind the trellis, if he got that far.

Your house is dangerous, sir. You ought to leave it until we find Albright. I'm authorized to offer you a place of safekeeping.

There are a half dozen fallacies in the logic of your offer. The most glaring is you don't have a place of safekeeping. Wait. I think I see where this is headed. You get me out of the house and capture Albright the next time he comes. You think Albright has kidnapped your watchman or dispatched him. Right?

I'm not authorized to divulge the plans of the agency.

Fair enough. Do you like fables?

Whatever is useful. Not if it's just a game.

It's not a game. It begins with the owner departing his house. The wolf is at the door. The owner's brave protectors stay behind to confront the interloper. When the creature appears, the leader of the woodsmen approaches. The leader feels an uncanny pull toward the open jaws of the beast, but he knows the talismanic word. Raven, he shouts. He disappears. One after another the woodsmen run to defend their leader, all shouting raven. They disappear. The Burgermeister has the property condemned, the house razed, the garden leveled and soon gone to weed, the gardener gone, they don't know where.

Why doesn't shouting raven work?

Because it worked only for Eric Nordquist. For anybody else it was fatal. And besides, you and your men would be thinking of the bird, a fatal confusion. Tell your superiors the home of Thomas Meachem is like the House of Nordquist. It doesn't have the same ghastly grandeur or the confusing shape of a ship, but it's just as dangerous.

We'll meet Albright in another place.

I can't wish you success.

* * *

You haven't said much about Eric, Ms. Albright.

I didn't see E hardly ever. I wasn't allowed in the studio, and he never came up on the hill. Paul said he saw him far from the house only once, down at the beach, but it must've been the only time, so he could attract Paul.

You spent a lot of time with Deirdre in the garden. I suppose she had become something of a mother to you.

I can see why you might say that, but it wasn't me she was mothering. Anyway, I didn't want a mother. I had gotten to be the wild child of the town, motherless, fatherless. I liked it that way. My hair was a big plus for wildness. I could run through the woods and catch things in it, spider webs and cottonwood fluff and maple spinners. I never let anybody brush it.

The nature of your relationship with Deirdre seems complex.

I wouldn't have spent any time with Deirdre if it hadn't been for Paul. I had to know whatever she knew. Didn't I tell agent number one about the thing that Deirdre was hiding from me?

No. I'd be interested.

It was like a half hidden mirror. I figured if I could get it turned the right way I'd look in it and know what was going on, but I never could do it. I told Paul about it, but he thought it was an hallucination.

Places like the House of Nordquist can give people strange thoughts, which is not to say that they are totally illusory.

So you've had cases like this before?

Yes. In every case we have to separate fact from fiction.

What about almost facts, things that almost happened?

They have to be eliminated. For instance, you have said you almost became Deirdre's Alicia, but you didn't.

That was just so I could find out what was going on. Alicia never sounded right to me. Sometimes I think the main thing Deirdre wanted from me was my hair.

Your hair.

Sometimes she would put her hand on it. I let her. She wanted to paint it. It matched something wild in her. Some Irish thing. Maybe she was pretending I was one of those children that are brought up in the wild by animals. What do you call them?

Feral children. But none have ever been proven to have been raised by animals.

I figured.

If you think there was a wild element in Deirdre, maybe we should consider again the possibility that she started the fire.

Wouldn't be my guess, but I was thinking of something else. What you said about Alicia and me.

Tell me. I'm interested.

Paul said that names are arbitrary. But it's more than that. What he didn't say is that even a short name like Alice is made up of parts that don't always stick together. Have you ever heard a yodeling stutterer?

No.

I don't mean the ones that go bub bub bub or the ones that sound like they're choking to death. I mean one like we had in our town a while back that sounded like she was yodeling from the top of a hill. And whatever she was yodeling got broken up by the wind before it got to you. So you just got pieces and had to try to fit them together. It made you sad because she really wanted you to hear what she was saying. So if you say my name, Alice or Alicia, you can feel the parts in your mouth. You don't have to yodel it. Go ahead. Say it.

You say it and I'll listen for the parts.

Oh I forgot. You can't ever call me by my first name. But this wouldn't be really calling me by name. It would be just practicing certain sounds. Or you could say No-Name. That's not against the rules, is it?

We'll talk about names later. I'd like to go back to the few times you saw Eric.

I didn't see him hardly ever, but I smelled him a lot. That's how I knew when he was near.

I wouldn't have guessed that he was odorous.

He was layered.

Layered.

The bottom layer was skin. The next layer was sweat. Actually there was no need to sweat in the basement of the House of Nordquist because it was always clammy and cold, but E sweated. The next layer was men's cologne. Deirdre must have ordered it for him from a catalog. There was always a lot of stuff being delivered.

Paul's letters don't mention any shipments other than musical equipment.

Because that's all he had to deal with. The rest was food and clothes and household goods. They ate a lot of queer stuff like fish out of wood boxes. I think one reason the house burned so fast was all the empty crates and cartons they must've put in the basement. I never saw where. Ritter at the hardware store told Paul that when the old man was alive they ordered gold braid for his admiral uniform. Deirdre must've sewn it on. I bet one of the scavengers found some melted gold in the ashes.

That's interesting. Cologne. Eric sounds like a person very hard to pin down.

You didn't try to pin E down. You just experienced him. Paul never pinned him down. To Paul E was a magic thing flying through the air with a red mane made out of fire like a gas station horse.

Maybe Professor Tyree pinned him down.

I think, reading the letters, if you could get through the high-falutin words, he got some things right about E. But I doubt he ever actually saw E. He was only there a day and a night before he got caught in the fire.

You tried to get Paul free of Eric.

It didn't work. Not then, not now. Not for the last twenty years. All that time he was waiting for a call from E whether he knew it or not.

Yes, we believe he's probably searching for Eric.

All this is pretty much a downer, isn't it. You want me to tell you something funny about E?

That would be welcome. It's hard to think of Eric as funny.

E's hair had split ends. Don't ask me how I know. I don't know if you have a wife. Even if you do, as a male you might not know about split ends. By the way, do you have any female detectives?

We do, but for sessions like this we don't match genders. Anyway, I don't know about split ends.

I don't mind not being matched. OK, I'll explain to you what split ends are. Split ends look like the frayed pieces where a tree branch gets broken in a storm. They're usually caused by the sun or a hair dryer that's too hot. But neither one of those could explain E's split ends. Maybe the heat of the synthesizer. I don't think Helene's hair had split ends. It was too tight on her head. My hair never has split ends because it doesn't have ends. It grows in circles. I used to brush Paul's face with it like some old movie temptress, Joan Crawford, but hers was as black as Helene's. My hair isn't any color.

Paul loved your hair. It's in the letters. You once said Eric's hair reminded you of fire. That takes us back to the hypothesis that Eric burned the house down.

Who knows. Who knows what E was. In the old movies a full moon would go behind the clouds and come out again and the main character would start to grow long hair and fangs and then you'd know for sure what he was.

* * *

*Dear Paul,*

*OK, I'm back from you don't know what or where, just like I don't know exactly what or where you are. I'm getting the hang of this letter writing. Tomorrow I'm going to write my son.*

*I'm going back to the night of the fire. We're in bed in the cottage your father left you. I'm in a death struggle with E for you. Over the bed the face of E is shining in the air with his red hair hanging down all over us like a double image in an old movie. All I have is my hair and my mouth and the rest of my body. I don't know how to use them. Everything's trial and error. I don't understand what E has. A machine that sucks up the sounds of Helene's body and wraps them around you like an octopus. Slick. But not like sweat. I know I can't ever cool off or I would lose you. I have to keep myself warm and creamy. How do I do it? I don't know.*

*We hear a lot of noise. Sirens. We let go of each other. To tell you the truth I'm relieved, because I can't come. I have to pretend. And now you're down in the City looking for him. You hate the City. That other Professor taught you that. City of Cain. I feel sorry for you. Twenty years with the wrong woman. The wrong dream.*

*Back to the fire. We ran up the hill. The fire engine couldn't get up the driveway. They shot water from their tanks up in the air. The wind blew it away, but it wouldn't have done any good anyway, not the way that fire was burning. I had an evil thought, which was don't let E get out. Or was it evil? I put that question in here because I don't want to fool around in this letter the way I fool around with the agents. Funning them, as my Daddy would say. I don't know why I do. And you're down in the City because you think E may not have burned up. You got a number on the phone. You think you're going to find him.*

*Before that night of the fire I had already dreamed I ran up the hill with a torch. That kind of dream can make you go crazy. It happens to young people in lots of movies. Guilt. You mix up wishing something and doing it. But I didn't want to torture myself so I said to myself if you live in a house with a room full of live wires and a machine full of blinking lights a fire is what you deserve.*

*We didn't see anybody running out. But the fire made our eyes water, so we could've missed it. The agent says there's a set of remains missing but they don't know whose. I'm not going to say any more about my son running out with the letters and going back in. That would only come between us again. Anyway, I don't know if the agents really know what they are talking about or if they just say things to see if they can spring something out of you. So go ahead. Keep looking for him. But I hope you don't find him. That's not sour grapes. It's because I don't want you to suffer. Because if you find him, he's not going to be flying across the beach like his feet aren't touching the ground and his hair is on fire, all to the sound of a great symphony. It would be terrible for you to see what he is now. He might be scorched. He might have been hiding in a basement all these years and never cut his hair or beard, which is now the color of ash. He won't be able to stand the light when you open the door. His eyes are all mattered up like an old dog. He won't recognize you.*

*You won't be able to stand the smell. You'd be better off coming back home. But then you'd always be wondering, wouldn't you?*

*And me. What was I doing for twenty years? I couldn't make a life out of remembering the House of Nordquist. Some morning I might try remembering what it was like down in the draw leaning against our trees. I didn't want to go back down there. Like E, it would be changed. Different brambles and vines. It might've been down there I conceived my two sons. Anyway, you can't go back. But one morning I made the mistake of playing Alicia. I went up on the hill. I didn't look at the burnt ruins. I could barely see the place where the garden had been. It was all overgrown. I tried to conjure up Deirdre, but it didn't work. Which reminds me of when that woman came to town and I decided to be a medium. You said it was OK with you, because you never worried it was going to work.*

*Another paragraph. How do you know when it's another paragraph? Never mind. I was getting cards from my older son, which was not the one I wanted to get mail from. The little stories he cramped onto the cards could be scary, especially at first, but then I saw that he was really good at getting out of tight places, like Errol Flynn or Douglas Fairbanks, Jr. And in my spare time, which was all of it, I was thinking things over. I won't ask you again how you felt about Professor Tyree coming to the House of Nordquist. Like a moth to a candle. He loved you and he loved the idea of E at the same time, which doomed him. In those letters to him you made the symphony and E sound exciting even when you were telling him not to come. I read the letters before I gave them to the agent. I'm never going to read them again, not because they're untrue. Everybody has a right to their version of the story. But once is enough. I got the picture.*

*And then I made you sit with me in the kitchen by the candle and drink wine and go over it, but nothing much new came out. I wouldn't enjoy any more talks like those. In fact I probably won't be here if you come back, but I haven't decided for sure yet. I'll miss agent number two. He gets me to say things I didn't know were in my head.*

*I'll write a letter to my older son too. They'll say, but you don't have his address. So what? He has a good life. You go from one famous place to the next. You see everything worth seeing. When the people start to get suspicious of you, you get back on the road. Wherever you show up next, nobody knows anything about you. Not like around here, where we stayed too long, where everybody knows me. The wife of the man that disappeared into himself after the fire. Madeline at the post office where I go to see if I got another card, Bobbi at the salon who admitted there was no reason for me to come to her because nobody even in Hollywood could do anything with my hair, old man Ritter's son Otto, Priss at the drugstore. Everybody remembers the fire even if they weren't born yet.*

*How do you end a letter from a wife to her husband if she doesn't know where he is exactly? And probably doesn't want her to know.*

~~*Sincerely,*~~
~~*All the best,*~~
~~*The best of everything,*~~
*Your loving wife. I'm sticking with that. The others are stiff, and this one is fluff, but I'm sticking with it.*

*Alice*

* * *

*Director*
*National Division A*
*A.P.O. D Box 3489*

*Dear Sir,*
*Let me introduce myself: Thomas Meachem, citizen, United States of America, currently residing in New York City. I am writing to offer information about the disappearance of three of your agents here in the City, their disappearance coming, as you know, after the disappearance of a guard posted at my house. I regret to say that I am reasonably certain that they will not be reporting back for duty. I believe that you will not see them again nor discover any remains. Their disappearance, while certainly not willful, is due to avoidable*

*error. I tried to make their leader aware of the risks involved in their search for Paul Albright. This account will be full. It will take me several sittings, for I find it fatiguing to write about ambiguity and errancy. I need time to enjoy the refreshment of my garden. It did not refresh your agent.*

*I request that you not seek from me further reflections on this unfortunate matter. I will have nothing more to say.*

*I am aware that other of your staff have had extensive conversations with Alice Albright about the fire that destroyed the House of Nordquist. I will avoid repetitions so far as I am able, based on the accounts of the agent assigned to interview me and on my conversations with Albright. Nevertheless I need to assure myself that we share certain elements of background information. Paul Albright and I were classmates at Justin and James College for Men, graduating in 1979. History was kind to us: too young for the Vietnam draft lotteries. I know that you, sir, are a much decorated war hero and reached the rank of three-star general before becoming head of your particular arm of national intelligence. I hope that you will not find offensive my reference to a kindly circumstance of history. I will be frank. I would have made an ineffective and reluctant soldier. So would Paul Albright.*

*Paul, if not brilliant, was a model student, nonpareil in his use of language, less so in the intricacies of thought and even less so in mastery of numbers. Some of the students called him St. Paul. So long as the moniker signified a mild saintliness and a mastery of the epistolary form (our writing assignments often took the form of imaginary letters, e.g., Sophocles to Hamlet) it was appropriate; but to the extent that it might have referred to the extraordinary energies of the famous evangelist, it was off the mark. Paul was not fervent in that way. It may seem odd to you that I take up this matter of Saul of Tarsus in these times when accounts of his teachings and famous travels are of little interest to most of our younger citizens. But at our college we had a magisterial Professor of Religion, Karl Aptheker, a Lutheran with a large quantity of the same ferocious zealousness that characterized the founder of his sect. He was, as the Germans say, massig, not so much physically as intellectually. Consequently, a Christianity of the darker sort hung over the campus. So the nar-*

*rative of the erstwhile persecutor blinded by light, unhorsed on the road to Damascus and lying in the roadway listening perforce to the voice of God was never far from us. I will have occasion to return to the phenomenon of blinding light.*

*How is this pertinent? You will not understand how your agents lost their way unless you understand Paul Albright and his mental roots. I know that your researchers are unparalleled in their thoroughness, but if they had been perfect you would not have lost three agents and a watchman. Of course nothing is perfect. Consequently, where imperfection has consequences less severe than the consequences of inaction we must proceed and suffer lashes in a good cause. But where imperfection has dire consequences we must turn aside and find a different way. I do not know much about the directives your agent received from his superiors other than that they infused him with tenacity and determination, admirable but fatal.*

*I offer a very brief summary of the years following Albright's graduation from college. I got my account from Albright himself. I repeat it here for purposes of continuity and also to give you the opportunity to compare it with other accounts you have. Before he graduated from college Paul Albright suffered the death of his father, from whom he inherited a cottage on the Hudson River and other assets which, though not large, were sufficient to excuse him from the necessity of working for a living. The cottage was located a mile or so downhill from the house of an eccentric Norwegian by the name of Gunnar Nordquist, who had died a decade or so before Paul took up residence in the cottage. The son, Eric Nordquist, inherited the property and a good quotient of his father's eccentricities. With the help of his mother, a woman of Irish extraction, he set out to compose a massive musical work that would have at its base the sounds of the body of a maimed woman named Helene. I know no other name. Paul became entangled with these people despite the protests of his fiancée, Alice Coulter, later his wife. A professor who shared with Paul a deep mutual fondness and respect came as a guest to the House of Nordquist, as it was called. He was there only a day and a night before a fire of mysterious origin ravaged the property and burned to death its inmates, with the probable exception of one. The fire also destroyed all record of the great musical masterpiece that was to* have changed the world, or at least no record is known to be extant, with the possible exception of a book of paintings by Eric Nordquist's mother, if it is to be credited that one can preserve a symphony in the form of pictures, or perhaps some system of graphic notation.

Your agency's research has no doubt unearthed much that I am not privy to, but it did not succeed in revealing knowledge sufficient to save your agents. Would such knowledge have enabled them to reach Albright and discover what of the origins of the conflagration and its consequences he knows? Might it have enabled them to accompany him or at least follow him in his quest for a person he believed escaped the holocaust? You will have to make your own judgment about these hypothetical possibilities.

I understand that your agents have spoken at length with Alice Albright. From my second hand knowledge of her I suspect she will have proven a difficult witness, a deeply emotional woman who observed the events in question and recorded them in memory with extreme sensitivity. She has been a devotee of Hollywood films, particularly old reruns. If the experience of your agents has agreed with what has been reported to me, you may well conclude that in her case factual narrative often shades off into an imaginatively reconstructed account. Indeed Albright revealed to me that she had conceived two imaginary sons, one of whom she averred was lost in the fire, or survived the fire. Albright could not make clear to me the exact nature of these contradictory reports because they were not clear to him. He said that at various times she understood and did not understand that the sons were not real. I must leave it at that.

So much for what we already share. In many basics the muchness lies in your favor. In my next installments I will try to make clear the parts of the story the understanding of which lies in my favor, the ignorance of which eventuated in the loss of your agents. You will include my account in your database. I hope it will remain safe there, but if you in your loss of personnel will forgive me, I must say that it amuses me that we use old metaphors to signify the lurking villains of the digital age—topless towers of data brought low by Trojan horses, monumental corpuses of information corrupted by worms and trolls. When I have completed all the installments of my report I will send them to you by snail mail, as they say, on paper *from which the ink will fade and whose fibers will be eaten away by acids.*

\* \* \*

No offense but I'm thinking about taking a trip.

I could tell from the minute you came in that something had happened.

Something came to the kitchen window at last. Don't ask if it had wings and shined in the dark, OK?

All right. I won't ask.

What about the agency? I mean my going on a trip.

The agency has no objection.

You mean as long as I come back?

There are no conditions.

You figure there's nothing more to get out of me.

You've been very helpful, Ms. Albright.

Ha. You almost said Alice, didn't you? I saw it right there on the tip of your tongue like a little frog about to jump off, but you swallowed it. Well Alice likes to tell the whole truth. She's not just thinking about a trip. She's thinking about leaving.

I'll bet there's a story behind that.

Not much of one. I've always wondered where people end up when they leave without knowing exactly where they're going. Destination Zero. It's the name of a movie about truck drivers. There's a gun in the glove compartment. Do they allow you to go to movies?

Sure.

What about guns?

I don't have one. Tell me about your trip

It's an old movie with John Garfield the gangster and Ida Lupino, who is playing the part of the moll Alice. Her mother named her after the song, Alice Blue Gown. The cabin of the truck is filled with cigarette smoke. Outside, the fog is so thick you can't see past the gas cap. Remember the old gas caps with winged gods?

I think they were radiator caps.

OK, radiator cap. This one is simple, just a round cap. How fast should you drive? You want to put miles between you and the last town, where the village idiot that works at the general store recognized you. But you could hit a deer and not be able to get away. There's headlights way back in the rear view mirror. The rear license plate number is scrubbed with steel wool, but that won't do any good. You don't know for sure who they are. You don't want to have to shoot it out. You want to make it to the motel with a diner next door that has a blinking neon sign that says Eat, Eat, Eat. You want to park behind the building.

Maybe Alice has the suspicion she'll meet somebody she knows there, somebody from her past.

I think you're on to something, but let me finish. In the diner the gangster and his moll Alice take the booth farthest from the door. He keeps the brim of his hat down so low that the camera has a hard time catching the worry lines on his face. The hat is worn and soft. The moll Alice has a little hat with a fuzzy top knot that her mother knitted for her when she was still a virgin.

A trip of the kind you're thinking about, not a movie trip, takes planning.

The guy behind the counter is wiping it for the hundredth time. Nerves. It's making the gangster nervous. He could shoot the rag out of the guy's hand, but that wouldn't be smart. Alice orders something that's not on the menu. The guy says he'll make it special for her. He doesn't have an emergency button behind the counter to call the cops like in modern times.

I wonder if this is really a permanent move or more of an adventure.

Permanent. In one version of the movie Alice the moll ends up back home and understands how beautiful it is for the first time and everybody understands her. But the Alice on your tapes, if she came home again, would end up back at the kitchen table with the candle and the bottle of wine, looking out the window until it's dark and then the window is a mirror with nothing in it but her.

I'm guessing you have some special reason for making this trip.

You already guessed. I'm going to see my older son. But if you give me your address, I'll send you a card showing some of the highlights of the trip. I forgot to tell you I've learned how to write letters. It was easy.

Traveling alone can be hard, especially for a woman, unless you have plenty of money.

Paul's father set up a trust before he died. It's handy for me, but it was bad for him because it meant he didn't have to work. The hardware was just a temporary thing. Twenty years he could sit around and think about E and the fire.

We believe he's searching for someone and is getting close.

I told you, he'll be lucky if he doesn't find E.

You know, Ms. Albright, if what you're really going to do is look for Paul you could wait a while and we'll have him for you.

I told you, I'm going to meet my older son.

But you don't know where he is.

I don't know where anybody is that matters. But I'll find him.

From what you've told me you might have to go to some dangerous places.

You forgot to say especially dangerous if you're a woman. But it doesn't matter. I'll find him.

What makes you so sure?

You promised you weren't going to ask any questions, but I'll answer anyway. Because there's no such thing as parallel lines. They always meet sooner or later. Paul told me that. A Russian figured it out. Which is odd, given the size of Siberia. I might have figured it out for myself from the House of Nordquist. The old man tried to design it so that you couldn't figure out how to get from one room to another. But he couldn't keep all the halls from meeting sooner or later. Like in the old horror movies the heroine was bound to run into the ghoul in one of the corridors she kept stupidly exploring. Every exit is an entrance onto another stage. That was another thing Paul told me. But E wanted the whole world for his stage, no exits. How crazy can you get? Anyway, I'm not afraid of getting trapped in another play.

Sometimes a bit of fear can be a good thing.

I didn't mean it couldn't happen. I meant I wouldn't be afraid of it.

One of our primary concerns is to keep you safe, Ms. Albright.

I know what that means. You're going to put a tail on me. He better be good because by the time I get three miles from here nobody will have ever heard of me.

                                    * * *

*Director*
*National Division A*
*A.P.O. D Box 3489*

*Second Installment*

*This reports a visit from Paul Albright one afternoon about a week ago. I don't keep a calendar. My initial inclination is to say that Albright came in a pensive mood, but the idea of Albright having what we normally call moods is inaccurate. What I should probably say is that for this visit he occupied a certain stratum of memory, each stratum (how many I can't guess) having its own perceptual modality. I know that my ability to gauge such matters is limited, but it is necessary for me to try to convey the tone of Albright's delivery as well as its substance or you will not have his narrative in its entirety. And though I can obviously offer no absolute assurance, I want to assert that the strangeness of what you read here comes from the principal and not the reporter.*

*On this visit Albright reported to me that shortly before the fire our old Professor John Tyree arrived at the house and was put up by Deirdre in a room in the basement. All the rooms in the house were below deck, so to speak, the main deck and the superstructure being reserved for nautical functions. Why did Professor Tyree and Albright not meet immediately upon Professor Tyree's arrival? Timing was of the essence, it seemed. Albright used the phrase the acceptable time (a frequent theme of another professor of ours) but did explain what determined proper timing. In any case the meeting never took place, the prospect of it lost in the conflagration along with everything else of that ill-fated house. In any case, the day of Professor Tyree's arrival Deirdre told Albright that the Professor was weary and would meet him the next day. At the same time she delivered to Albright a packet containing his letters to Professor Tyree. If that seemed in any way ominous to Albright, he did not say so. But the delay in meeting with his old Professor did prove trying for Albright, who was very anxious to see and speak to Professor Tyree. He had decided to urge that they both leave the House of Nordquist immediately and never return. They would at the same time liberate Alice.*

*I listened with care to the account of this surprising resolve, Director, because I knew how hard it would be for Albright to separate himself from Eric. I pressed him. He said that matters in the studio had become ever more menacing. There was never now any utterance. Albright received his instructions along cold waves of intentionality that beat against his consciousness with the force of a storm driven sea—his phrase. He wondered if it was the same with Helene, but she lay still on the stone. He could only know for certain that they shared the word, or sound, raven. It floated unspoken in the air above them, passing from one to another of the four black sarcophagi.*

*His instructions, he said, were rigidly clear. He, No Name, was to stand in an exact spot in front of an oscilloscope and monitor the amplitude of the base harmonic and if necessary adjust input to keep it constant. There were numbers, but I've forgotten them. He was not to worry about the amplitude or frequency of the lesser partials shown on the screen. This troubled him. In his mind, a mind as we know almost constantly metaphorical, he associated Alice, Professor Tyree, and Deirdre with the diminished partials, all overborne by Eric's manipulation of Helene's major, which was itself paradoxically composed of partials—the susurrus of rushing blood, the ringing of iron. The living were being subordinated to the dying. He regretted that he could not feel much compassion for Helene, but it was hard to identify with one who willingly gave herself up to complete immolation.*

*And now in Albright's account there came back his old predisposition to poetry. He said he wanted to cry out to Eric: how can you make a symphony out of arbitrary waves, intervals tumbling back and forth like empty shells along an uneasy shoreline, the whistling of the wind rising and falling according to your cruel whims? That outcry was never of course articulated in Eric's studio but only in my little gazebo in the middle of my garden.*

*Raven not the bird. Strange, is it not, Director, that a word not only familiar but also rich with poetic associations could be stripped of its referent, converted into a constantly modulating signal and set sailing through a space defined by its own motion.*

*I earnestly hope that I am succeeding in conveying to you, as Albright conveyed to me, the extremity of distress and distortion he was feeling ever more intensely. The detailed exactness of his memory is extraordinary. He has kept it for a quarter of a century in a vault impenetrable by the worms of forgetfulness. The intensity of his recall acts upon the listener as a dread attraction, like some huge presence speeding close by and pulling one into its wake.*

*It is this man, with these attributes, whom your agents went in search of. Who could have prepared them?*

*End of Second Installment.*

* * *

*Dear Son,*

*I've been wanting to write you for a good while. I wrote my husband before, but this is harder. For one thing I'm not good with names, not even my own. Anyway, I was going to save this for later in the letter, but it wants to come out now. It's about Deirdre's paintings in the big black book you went back into the house to save from the fire. Nobody knows where the book and the paintings are. The paintings show Eric's music that came out of Helene's body. Can you paint music? There are agents here who would love to get their hands on the book. They keep asking me about it, to the point where I'm* not sure anymore whether I ever saw the paintings or not. I told my husband I remembered one that looked like a twisted body. Deirdre talked about this new way of painting she learned from Eric. She called it painting from the inside. It gave me the creeps.

The agents ask a million questions about the fire. Was it an accident? Who started it? Where? Who got out? What did they get out with? Where are they now? The questions are the right questions, but they're not going to figure it out. It's not facts. It's what swirls around the facts, if that makes any sense.

Another reason I'm writing is to tell you I'm going away for a while, so if you were thinking about coming back for a visit I won't be here. The agents would love to talk to you and tape what you say, but I can tell you the sessions get boring. I don't think I'll come back. I don't mean I might get caught somewhere or that there would be something here I couldn't stand not to come back to. I mean that if you stay away from a place very long, it might not welcome you back, or it might not even be there anymore. That didn't happen to places in the past but it does now. I don't think my husband thought about that when he left. So I figured maybe it was my duty to stay here until he got back, just to keep the place steady, but he probably won't come back. He's looking for Eric. I wrote him he'll be lucky if he doesn't find him. He's got in mind the Eric that was in the story about the symphony, but people change, sometimes too much to bear.

You know my husband's old Professor was in the house at the time of the fire. I used to think of him as just a little hunchback twerp who could never have done anything but spin out words, words, words. Never could have started a fire. But now I'm not so sure. I don't know what you think.

On another note I wonder if you have heard from your brother. I thought I might try to nab him for a minute before he went speeding by. But I'd need at least some rough coordinates. I got that idea of lines around the earth from my husband. Once he and Eric were sailing the old man's ship toward the north pole and they had some coordinates, but they never got there. They got locked in ice. I don't think my husband's going to find what he's looking for this time either. He doesn't have the right coordinates.

*Listen. I know you must be busy, but think about dropping a line. It's been a long time.*

*Your loving mother Alice.*

* * *

*Director*
*National Division A*
*A.P.O. D Box 3489*

*Installment #3*
    *I resume my report of Albright's account of his work with Eric Nordquist. I understand that your agency must always aim at confirmation of the facts. I can assure you with a reasonable degree of certainty that I am reporting to you accurately what Albright said. I can offer no confirmation of the facticity of his accounts other than to emphasize the passion and the vividness with which he delivered them to me.*
    *Your agency has set itself the task of finding Albright and getting the facts directly from him. You have lost four men in this endeavor. No doubt you hesitate to commit more. This raises an interesting question that you have no doubt thought about. How is it that I am immune to his deadly ambience? I don't know. A certain concatenation of flowers, a tutelary spirit in the form of an ageless Japanese gardener, the protective arch of an intricately vined trellis, a hat as old as music. I am not being frivolous. In the case of a fatal interior of the kind your men entered, we have to assume that I have a talisman of safe passage, though I don't know what it is. Your agents did not have a talisman.*
    *To go on with Albright's narrative. Every day Deirdre delivered Helene to the studio with the same gliding grace of movement, royal handmaiden to her doomed queen. Albright, changing the metaphor, said she had the mien and manner of one of those courteous execu-*

tioners, always hooded, that appeared in many scenes of beheading in old England, receiving always the forgiveness of the condemned and perhaps a coin with a kingly face on it. Once before he had used an entirely different metaphor to characterize Deirdre. She was the Great Mother, who is incredibly fecund but disposes of her children as she pleases.

One day Albright heard Helene singing in the passageway just outside the door to the studio. This had not happened before. Hope leapt up in him. Something had freed her to sing her own song. She would no longer be shackled to Eric's stone and wires. She would change the nature of the symphony and the fate of the House of Nordquist. What was the singing like? It was pierced with a longing so deep that it summoned an attendant chorus, which alas sang an antistrophe—what happened at the crossroads had already happened and could not be undone.

Hardly a moment later, he said, raven flew in, its emanations like a pick-ax splintering ice. Now came the silent thrall and her escort, who having led her charge to the stone, proceeded to deliver to Eric a large black book. He opened it and for a short while studied several pages in silence. Albright saw fractionally, or imagined he saw tight loops of vary-colored lines, as if Deirdre had taken the images of the wires in the studio and the waves of the oscilloscope and the scintillances of the synthesizer and painted them as an inescapable coil of music. In his eye the painting was not still. He likened it to a helix of serpents spiraling upward into the cavernous dark of the studio. I have great difficulty constructing for myself even an approximate picture of what he saw.

At this point in his narrative, Director, Albright turned swiftly from a report of what he saw in the studio to what he felt inside himself. The connections between the two are obviously charged but not always perfectly clear to me. What was clear was the terrible disturbance he has carried within him all these years since the fire. I believe that disturbance has formed itself, all unwilled, into an unalterable intention that in turn has created the fatal spaces that are the reason for this communication. But I have wandered into speculation. I return to Albright.

*He got up from his chair. We were sitting in the small unwalled gazebo that my gardener had thatched for me. He walked out onto a path that rove among the flowers that surrounded us, but I could see that he did not cast his eyes among their colors, nor upward to the blue sky that favored us that day. Consequently, I can't report the physical or mental purposes of these breaks in his account, only that there were several. Perhaps they were merely a kind of punctuation, a long musical rest from which all resonance had to recede before he could go on into the next part of his account.*

*Seated again, Albright said that there in the studio he began to feel an ominous concentration throughout his body, a tight gathering about the heart. Groping for the right metaphor, he at last said that though he had never been a diver he knew that one must descend slowly to give the body time to deal with the added pressure. And one must ascend slowly to let the body decompress. But what medium was he in? It seemed oceanic, but it was not water. What was he descending toward? What did he hope to ascend to?*

*I render this portion of my report with great care for accuracy, Director, because the nature of Albright's metaphors seems crucial.*

*Well, he said, who was he to plumb the depth of such mysteries? He was merely No-Name, a gauge of amplitudes and intervals. His job was to signal to Eric when he was approaching the tolerances of his instruments—Helene, machine, speakers, the very walls of the studio. Albright's speech became excited, driven. He was a droplet of alchemical precipitate. If his insertion into a vial containing a concentrate of Eric's will turned it red, that signified that the elements of the great symphony had fused and were ready to be poured out upon the world, at which moment all of the operatives of the studio— No-Name, Helene, Deirdre, Eric himself— would be purged, useless dregs left after the universal transformation, to be cast into the fire. Raven not the bird would now cut with its huge pinions through the rotted world, a swift and ceaseless scything.*

*That must do it for this sitting, Director.*

* * *

I thought you might've left already.

You're funning me. Your man will report to you when I've left. Actually I was just about to, but I remembered I never told you Helene's story.

We didn't know you'd ever talked to Helene.

I didn't need to talk to her. The story's interesting but it has some holes in it. Like the countries she was in are never named. Anyway, you've heard the basic story and would've seen it in the movies a hundred times if you went to the movies. Before the family could leave, her husband was shot dead. It was mountain country so she and her two boys took his body to the top. The dogs wouldn't go there to gnaw on the corpse, not even birds. It was that cold. And there were ice gods around. The sun shined there a lot, but just for light, not heat. You could put the body up on a table of stones and go up there a hundred years later and the flesh would be kind of like brown glass with the bones shining underneath, pure white, all two hundred and three of them.

Amazing.

Later of course the boys were flushed out and put to work on munitions. She never saw them again. They put her on a train. Hundreds were crammed in cattle cars. The soldiers threw the personal bags out to make more room, so everybody left with nothing.

She could've replaced the sons if she'd wanted to. There were plenty of motherless children on the train if you wanted one or more. They had been lifted up into the cars from the platform. All you could see was hands reaching out and faces. All the bodies were out of sight.

Terrible.

As a child I used to think trains were nice. You had to go across the river if you wanted to stand by the tracks, but you could hear them tooting from our side if the wind was right. I got ready to have a nightmare about her story. The faces and hands wouldn't have bodies. When they got them up into the car they would put them in straw and hope they would grow bodies again. If they didn't, the soldiers threw them in pits to be eaten by lye because they couldn't work.

But you didn't have the nightmare.

No but I might as well have because I'd already had it just thinking of the story. The train she was on got hijacked by a band of guerillas or some other group in all that confusion and they turned it west. It went downhill to the ocean. She got to some island surrounded by water and stayed there a long time. Then she came to America. They gave her to Deirdre. They thought Deirdre was a nun, so they skipped the paperwork. That's how she escaped your database.

Many did. We have much work to do.

That's what I thought you'd say, because everybody knows No-Names are all around, in shacks and rusted out mobile homes, under highway bridges, in the state parks of warm states.

It's hard to believe Helene never had any qualms about coming to the House of Nordquist.

It was because of Deirdre. She might look like she's just gliding around, and her words might never go up and down, but it's like standing too close to a train. You get pulled in. Helene got pulled in.

Later, though, Helene surely had second thoughts, maybe about escaping the House of Nordquist.

Helene didn't have thoughts, as far as I could tell. She just lay down on the stone with the wires and gave it all up.

Eric and his mother made a powerful team.

I'll tell you something about that. One time in the kitchen looking through the candlelight I asked Paul if he remembered the time we danced naked in the woods. He said he didn't. If he'd said he did he would've been lying, because I made it up. But that doesn't mean I didn't want to dance. I wanted to dance the house down. I wouldn't have cared if it came down on top of my head or if I danced myself to death as long as I brought the house down, but I couldn't have danced hard enough to bring that place down. Nobody could. Fire was the only thing that could bring it down.

Everything leads back to the fire. We believe Paul will find who he's looking for and we'll know more about the fire.

That would be fine with me.

You said you weren't going to look for Paul.

That's right.

I wonder what your reaction will be if we find them together.

Who? Paul and E?

Or Paul and the Professor.

What would my reaction be? Not much. They've been together for twenty years.

⁜ ⁜ ⁜

*Director*
*National Division A*
*A.P.O. D Box 3489*

*Installment #4*

*I interrupt briefly the narrative of Albright's activities in Eric's studio in order to establish more firmly Albright's condition and his state of mind when he arrived here in the city. It may not seem necessary to you to return to these beginnings but I feel the need to ground the story once more in the circumstantial. Otherwise it begins to slip into the fantastical.*

*Albright arrived here in the City with nothing but a number. Numbers are fickle. In the judgment of your agent, however, the number was a precise clue with a referent that, once identified, would lead to the location of Albright. It was futile to try to convey to him a sense of the shiftiness of numbers. After many forceful petitions on his part I reluctantly gave him the number that had appeared on my doorstep. I believed it would lead him into a benign labyrinth. Albright would not be in the center. Meanwhile, I thought, the walking of the labyrinth might lead to useful reflections on the complexity and perils of pathways. He came back to report that the number had led to an empty location in the Arctic Ocean. Before that he reported a visit to the house of an old woman, where he found evidence of a visit from Albright. I suspected that he was mistaken about that and told him so, but he persisted in the belief that he had come close to Albright.*

*It was not, however, a number that undid your errant four. What undid them was disbelief. It is hard to blame them of course. Who can easily believe in the existence of a space contiguous to no other space and in the perfection of its interiority intolerant of entry. It may be that some others besides Albright have gone into such a space and come back, great mystics clothed in garments of indestructible faith. But such were not your agents, their leader being quite pure in his dedication to rationality. I admire his fidelity, fatal though it was.*

*The loss of your men sometimes lies heavily on my conscience. I should have been more emphatic, more reasonable. I fear that the lead agent took me for a mere eccentric, my warnings the product of an overheated imagination. Anyway I apologize if the rehearsal of this matter seems redundant. It has probably been more for my benefit than yours, to remind me that, as strange as the narrative has been, it is not as strange as what is to come.*

*I resume. The next time Albright entered my garden he did not walk normally. His gait was marked by a stutter step, as if the ordinary continuum of space was constantly interrupted. I invited him into the garden as before. Here my gardener had newly created a small pond and planted the shore with tiny bonsai pepper trees. Albright paused at the archway, looking up into the thick vines that wind around the trellis. I felt sure he was contemplating its metaphorical potential. It reminded me that in college Albright often declined to accept a simple relationship between signifier and signified. For example, the beret that always covered Professor Tyree's pate, indoors and out, we students assumed was simply a headpiece to hide cranial deformity. But Albright probed its black undulations for a deeper significance. What have you discerned, Saint Paul, we wanted to know. A mystery, he said, smiling enigmatically. We believed he could articulate the mystery if he chose because his mastery of words was already rising near the level of the Professor's, but he declined. We thought that perverse, but reflecting on the matter now, I'm inclined to believe that for Albright the mystery of the black beret* was truly ineffable, an early enigma in a series that has over many years formed the character of the elusive personage we now call Paul Albright.

Eventually we passed beneath the vines without comment. He was clearly more heavily burdened than on his previous visits. I tried to imagine the strenuous effort of investing one's self in one charged space and then another, each different, each without discernible dimensions, none connected to another. I could not imagine it though I knew it to be the case. Your agents could not credit it. I ushered Albright into the garden, hoping that the quietness and the gentle symmetries of the place might lighten his load. As we strolled the garden I stole glances at him. I managed to see, through the weight of the memories that burdened him, the Paul of our college days. He was at that time a beautiful creature, beautiful, not handsome, more faun than Adonis, and like a faun never quite fully formed.

On the wandering path he stopped, surveyed the flowers and said that the garden was beautiful but not the center. I said that nothing we know is the center. He said that our Professor of Religion, Aptheker, would say that there is a center, only we cannot experience it. Just at this moment in my writing my mind turns to your tireless labors in behalf of the safety of us all. I know that at a concealed locus your staff gathers and your supercomputers categorize and hypothesize, reaching for the high probability required for concerted action. But it can never find the center. Aptheker was right about that. In the final analysis you have to proceed on the basis of a local thickening of contingencies around a carefully constructed hypothesis. In the great majority of cases you obviously succeed. In the case of Albright you have not, cannot. He does not exist along the ordinary spectrum of likely and improbable, centered and decentered. His is a different passage. I cannot describe it. That inability of mine has lost you four men. I regret that deeply.

My thoughts turn now from your work to Eric's. They are profoundly related. I mean no offense. As I understand it, Eric intended to create in his studio, from a human body that bore witness to a culmination of historical evils, a new pattern for reality. You intend to shine the pure light of reason on the fiery destruction that ensued at the House of Norquist. No doubt you ask yourself whether the subterranean powers of that place, encapsulated by the supra-lingual raven, is waiting somewhere to return, as they say the bacillus of the plague is always with us in some fragment of flesh in a shallow grave.

Albright and I continued along the path the gardener has created, leading from the intense green of mosses, ferns, and dense bamboos to a place of deepening blue, simple corn flowers, clematis, vibrant irises, then to the other end of the spectrum—daisies, goldenrod, chrysanthemums, day lilies and finally a row of salmon and burgundy roses. These bursts of color are alien to a Japanese garden, but my gardener is compliant. There was a period of my life when I needed a via negativa, a reductio ad silentium. Now I prefer a restrained plenitude. But this report is not about me. When I resume, the focus will be sharply on Albright, but I thought it useful to depict more fully the subject and his effect on the mind of his interlocutor.

* * *

Dear Paul, Last Letter,

I'm back, you don't know where from again. I'm getting ready to go, this time for good. I've got a number out west and my credit card. Thanks for that. I thought I better tell you about how I'm leaving the house and all that. I'm leaving all the papers and letters, including my letters to you on your desk. The agent has made a copy of everything. Still, I bet they'll sneak in here when I'm gone. If you ever come back and find them here, just invite them out, if you can. They're not much fun to talk to.

Last night I said good-bye to the kitchen. You've got a few more suppers from the candle, so I didn't replace it. And besides, with all that dripping wax, it looks interesting, like it's from a pirate movie. I used everything out of the refrigerator or threw it away and then I turned it off, but it seemed so lonely in its silence I turned it back on. In the window was only my face. Nothing outside was moving. Not a breeze, and the ash was as still as if Deirdre had painted it in her old days. Well I guess you can't expect everything to keep on swaying just *in hopes that somebody will come back. Still, I wouldn't have minded at least a little good-bye wave. It was like my leaving didn't matter.*

*Like I said, I've got this number out west to find my older son, the world traveler. I'm going to find him whether he wants me to or not. Anyway, he's all I've got at the moment, which is OK because some people don't have anybody. You see it in the old movies, a bare light bulb hanging from the kitchen ceiling, an empty whiskey bottle and some cigarette butts. You can almost smell it. But that won't happen if you're on the move. That's me now. I thought about coming down to the City and delivering my letters to you. You can hide from the agents, but you can't hide from me. I've got too good a nose. It could be fun, walking up and down all those long blocks with every known type of people and goods. But I decided against it.*

*You remember that woman Eric had, Helene? Of course you do. Well, it came out in one of those boring sessions with the agent that she had a husband and two sons that got killed before she left the old country, Germany. Anyway you and I were thinking she might be a virgin that was being sacrificed, remember? Sometimes we were like children making up a story to play parts in. Anyway, what difference did it make if you were a virgin or not, lying on a cold stone day after day. I don't know why I thought of this. Virginity doesn't mean much to men. Just the first time.*

*That's it. I hope when you find what you're looking for it's what you really want. But watch out what you wish for, you might get it, the old saying goes.*

*Your loving wife,*
*Alice*

\* \* \*

So you're all packed.

Yes. I thought you might try to stop me so I've got a pistol in my purse.

Luckily, Ms. Albright, I've gotten to know your sense of humor.

That's just one more reason for me to leave. I'm out of jokes.

I believe we're going to wind this case up soon.

By winding up you mean the facts?

In the final analysis, the facts are all there is.

You might know the fact, who struck the match, but still not know who really started the fire.

You're selling us short, Ms. Albright. Why the person struck the match, who might've influenced him or her are also facts. But we go back only so far. Otherwise we get caught in a chain of infinite regress until we're back to the Big Bang.

Paul told me about the Big Bang. At first I thought he was kidding. Anyway, according to his religion professor you don't have to go back to the Big Bang. You only have to go back to the Garden of Eden, because there was nothing human before that. It reminds me of the butterfly in Mexico theory Paul told me about.

I'm not familiar with that theory.

The butterfly flaps its wings in Mexico and causes a hurricane in Galveston. I've never been to Galveston. But the town is in a song about gulls flying in the sun. Better than a raven, which I keep forgetting was not a bird. Paul told me about that storm. The city never came back. It was one of those things Paul's mischievous classmates would bring up to their religion professor, why God would allow a storm like that and all those deaths. The Professor had an answer. I don't remember what it was.

Natural disasters are difficult for proponents of providence.

E thought he was providence itself, if I know what providence is.

Eric was obviously a megalomaniac.

Sure, and everybody had to do what he said. Helene had to give him her body, Deirdre had to paint the pictures and keep Helene alive, Paul had to be No-Name and turn the knobs and watch. I kept telling Paul that it was going to end bad, which was the same thing as telling the wind. That's one big reason I'm heading west. I've had to live with E and the fire and all that for twenty years. I figure I've got a vacation coming. Out where the buffalo roam and a friend is a friend.

And Paul is getting away too.

I'm surprised you would say something tricky like that after all our time together. He's not getting away. He's looking for E. He's your key contact. I bet you've got tails on him twenty-four seven, as they say. You know the rules. If nobody testifies he saw the act, you have a hard time proving it happened. One thing, though, I never got in the movies was the corpus delicti thing. Why would you have to find the body if a bunch of people saw Jack murder Jill? Jack could've burned the body up and spread the ashes to kingdom come or sunk it in concrete in the middle of the Gulf of Mexico off his yacht.

It's not just the corpus dilicti we want to talk to Paul about.

I'm surprised you say that because all along you and the other agent have been talking about missing one of the corpuses dilicti.

Yes, we do hope Paul will lead us to the missing corpus dilicti, but our ultimate goal is to clear up the mystery of the fire.

OK, if you ever find Paul, which I doubt, he might lead you to the corpus dilicti hidden somewhere down there in the City of Cain, or he might not be able to find it himself.

We hope he will find it. We believe he will.

Speaking of hope, there's a going away present you could give me.

Name it.

Tell me what you think the facts are in that last kooky letter Professor Tyree wrote before he came to the House of Nordquist. It didn't sound like dreams to me.

He said the dreams were suppositional. I believe he meant they were half awake hallucinatory experiences. Nevertheless hallucinatory experiences are facts. That's not in dispute. What's much harder is to determine what elements within the hallucinations are themselves objective facts.

Well, which ones are?

We hypothesize that what he experienced was an extreme form of dislocation in time and space that distorted the objects of his perception. He experienced being in a place and seeing things he had only read described. Did the distortions contain some elements of fact? Maybe.

You want to know what I think?

Of course.

I think dwarves live in a world of their own like kids. There's a lot of holes in it, so you fill them up with things you imagine. And if you're good at words, you can write it all down and make it real.

That's very astute, Ms. Albright.

Holes in the world probably means holes in your database. It reminds me of a thing that happened to me when I was a child. You want me to tell you?

Yes I do.

OK. One time when I was a little girl named Alice Coulter we were playing Hide-and-Seek and I found a secret hiding place where the It couldn't find me. A deep closet piled up with winter clothes. They looked everywhere and couldn't find me, so I finally came out and shouted ha ha ha you couldn't find me. But there was nobody there. The game was over. I won. But there wasn't anybody out there. For a long time all I could find was scraps of the other children, like pieces of pictures cut out from a coloring book. I didn't think they would ever all come back. Maybe that was what happened to Professor Tyree. In his dream he came out of hiding and went to the House of Nordquist and the people weren't the ones he'd dreamed.

You are very insightful, Ms. Albright.

Ms. Albright again. I have had a bunch of names: Alice Coulter, Alice Albright, just plain Alice, Alicia, Ms. Albright. But no one has ever called me Mother. I wonder if E ever called Deirdre mother or if she was always just the one that would get him what he needed. Like the postcards from my wanderer son never have a named greeting like Dear Mother. They always just started off with a bang telling me about some adventure in a fabulous place.

Yes, you have spoken of your son before.

I know what you think about my sons.

We are holding them in suspension between imagination and fact.

How long can you hold them in suspension? Could you hold them in suspension twenty years?

If the case requires, even longer.

I don't think Professor Tyree could hold imaginings and facts in suspension.

Whether or not he could, the fire ended his confusion.

I don't think the fire ended much of anything. Maybe you ought to spend your time looking for the next House of Nordquist. But that's for you to decide. My job is to head west and find at least one son.

I wish you well.

Another thing. I told you about Paul and me talking in the kitchen.

Yes.

The candlelight was a big part of it. I could've told the Professor, or anybody else, if you have firelight you never know where it's going. In the kitchen the candlelight kept moving from the lantern on the table to the window and up on the wall and back. It could've burned the house down any time it wanted to, but it didn't. It was frustrating to me, our faces moving around from table to wall to window. It was hard enough to talk to Paul when you could keep him still for a few minutes.

Talking to a face in a window would be difficult.

He would say that I saved him from the fire even though he never listened to me at that time. I was somebody called Cassandra scratching my face with my nails and tearing my hair out by the roots, but nobody listened.

Paul must've listened. He escaped the fire.

Nobody escaped the fire. Paul is off looking for the one he thinks did. I don't think he'll find him. I don't think your men will find Paul.

I suspect you'll say it's because it's too late.

That's right. Double jeopardy, statute of limitations. The murderer can't be tried again, no matter what's been found, unless Humphrey Bogart tricks the murderer into a legal trap, mostly by talking like a machine gun with his teeth clenched. There's always a crack in the story. You know where the crack in this story is?

Tell me.

The crack is you can't make everybody believe you can suck a symphony out of a body and change the world with it.

That was the premise of the story all right. But it seems you were the only one who didn't believe it.

I think maybe the Professor had his doubts, but I could have told him he didn't need to set the house on fire to prove it.

So you now believe Professor Tyree started the fire.

It's a hypothesis. And now I'll excuse myself. I've told you and you predecessor all the facts I know, twice or more. I hope you find what you're looking for. I hope we all find what we're looking for.

* * *

*Director*
*National Division A*
*A.P.O. D Box 3489*

*Installment 5*

*In this installment I return to the House of Nordquist. Albright took up the strenuous narrative after he had sat silent for a while in my garden. At this point in the story the Professor had arrived and was lodged in a room in the basement of the House of Nordquist. Albright had just received from Deirdre the Professor's last letter recounting the two infamous dreams. I have not read it of course and have only Albright's account of it. I resist the inclination to call the letter an account of aberrant fantasies. You have a copy and will have made your own judgment. In any case, the disturbance the letter caused in Albright was great. He paused and said he wondered if these dream details were important to me. I assured him that whatever was important to him was important to me. He looked at me curiously. I think he was trying to understand, not for the first time, exactly why he was telling me the tale. A shadow passed over his face. But he went on.*

*Among the matters in the letter that arrested Albright was a passage in which the Professor wrote that Eric spoke the word raven and that it ignited in his ear. I have to confess that this series of Albright's visits has caused me to have a lurid experience with that utterance. Once when I was half asleep it went around and around in my head, tipping its wings and wheeling about to pass again and again through my mind, shining its black eye into mine. I did not reveal to Albright my experience with raven.*

*Albright returned to Eric's studio. He said that the signs that marked for him the decline of Helene came to him as self-contained phenomena. For example, her lowering herself gradually onto the stone and slowly rising again became a precise choreography of waning. She became more and more emaciated, but that was to him less a sign of morbidity than a striking revelation of anatomical features hitherto hidden—the rib cage now two perfectly delineated sets of symmetrical bone, the fragile articulation of the limbs lucid beneath the ever thinning flesh. Meanwhile the synthesizer, relaying diminished patterns to the oscilloscope, joining speaker to speaker with ligatures of broken legato, was now clearly the habitation of virtually all of the vitality that Helene had brought to the House of Nordquist.*

*Albright sensed that he was losing the ability to think what he ought to think, feel what he ought to feel. How morbid was the sensibility that focused precisely on details of motion and anatomy and not at all on fatal debility? Forcing himself to recall his basic humanity, he asked himself how this fellow creature, for days and days in extremis, was being kept alive. This urged him to think of acting in her benefit. But what should he do? Shout execrations at Eric and by this gesture of rebellion free himself and Helene from the coils of the machine? Unlikely. In fact, Eric might delight in the noise because it could stimulate Helene's lapsing body to release yet new skeins of torn music. Should he flee? Take Alice away from Deirdre, wrest Helene from Eric? To his dismay he could not will himself to act. His mind leaped instead to Professor Tyree's haunted dreams. Eric flew out of the dark, the fire of his head casting all about him a lurid glow. Behind him a yawning cave, like a reverse cornucopia, drew into its black maw all the detritus and offal of the world's history.*

*You may be thinking, Director, that Albright was as deranged as the Professor. And that may certainly be true, but there was, I speculate, a profound difference between the states of the two. Here is my view. The Professor was caught in a temporal disorder, a brokenness of time marked by a disorienting alternation of continuity and flashes of futurity. As a result he was sometimes paralyzed and at others impelled to act precipitously. At a college, where little is of great moment, these unresolved volte face can actually prove instructive to students and colleagues, but in a place like the House of Nordquist, they can cause one to act at just the wrong moment.*

*Now you may be expecting me to say that Albright, in contrast to Professor Tyree's entrapment in temporal confusion, was, and is, caught in a spatial disorder. That would be partially true, but an oversimplification. Albright is caught in a number of unique spaces. I have no name for them, or even any apt analogies. Here's a stab: the lingering silences that comes between movements in a symphony, silences that remain structured by what has gone before and by anticipation of what may come—structured but unwedded to any material object. As I told your agent more than once, these spaces do not form a series, respect no hierarchy, answer no predictive calls. Which is more terrifying, Director, to live in a world in which all the hands of all the clocks and all the digital dials whirr and whirr until they go up in flames, or to live in a world of discrete spaces empty of what one had hoped for and unenlivened by the longed for sound, raven? I speculate that if Albright had been destroyed by the fire and the Professor spared, your men in pursuit of the survivor would still have been in mortal danger. There is little practical difference between stepping across a spatial border that can never be re-crossed and stepping into a river of turbulent events that leads toward a cataract.*

*Well, what do I do with these scraps of understanding? I sit in my garden. I watch my gardener work his wonders under the shadow of his ancient hat. The shadow is not of a color or density you have ever seen. Mauve might be close. But much more important than my state of fractional understanding, is the question, what do you do, Director, with the incomplete data you have? You are responsible for maintaining order and guarding the safety of the citizenry. You declare that all crimes are solvable. If there are in the public record unsolved crimes, it is only because the evidence has not yet been assembled. What can I say? Caveat secutor. Do not pursue Albright. He is not the one you want. He was abed with his beloved when the fire started. Send your men out onto the streets of the City to search for the remains of the incomplete narrative of the fire. I believe that you have trained them to perfection. If only they do not insist on finding Albright, they will be rewarded. I see a haggard creature. In a voice like the screech of a rusty hinge he or she will tell all that there is left to tell. The telling will be riddling of course. Take it. There will be no more. You will know what to do with it.*

*I will have one more report for you, Director. I will not see Albright again. I dread what I must tell in my last installment. It will be long, because it must come unbroken from memory. It will seem fantastical. Perhaps it is fantastical. With Albright one begins to lose one's footing in reality.*

\* \* \*

I very much appreciate your coming to talk with me, sir.

I don't mind. Been wondering what you had in this rig. Been talking to Alice Albright, I believe.

That's right.

I wasn't sure I could walk up this hill. I'm between ninety-five and a hundred you know. My son could tell you exactly. He runs the hardware now. Miracle he can make a living off of it with that big depot place down in Allen's Mill, but he knows the business and people appreciate that. Albright would've made a good hardware man himself, but he didn't need the work. Quit after the fire. And now he's flown the coop, I hear.

Yes he's down in the City.

What's he doing down there?

That's what we're trying to find out.

And now Alice has left.

That's right. Just yesterday.

Wonder where she went.

Out west, I think.

On the bus. Must be to some one-horse town. My feeling is if a town ain't got a train station it could be good to skip it.

Do you mind, sir, if I tape our conversation?

Not at all, but you won't make a nickel out of anything I say. I gotta laugh at myself. I was hoping you would serve me a subpoena. Never seen one. My son says it's just a piece of paper, but I bet it's got a seal or notary on it. You sure you don't want to swear me in, hand on the Bible, state your full name?

That's not necessary, sir. We don't doubt you'll tell us the truth.

I will if I can, but some of the truths I once knew are way back there.

We believe you talked to Professor Tyree when he first came here.

The little dwarf?

Yes.

Came here the same day as the fire. I would say he was wrong-footed, by birth and by walking right into a big fire.

Yes. Could you tell me what passed between the two of you?

What passed between us was as much distance as I could keep. I didn't like the look of him.

But you gave him a ride up to the House of Nordquist.

That's right, because there he was standing on the siding where my goods had come in and asking me how he could get a taxi. I had seen him get off the train, which was quite a thing in itself, kind of a twist and a jump, with a little grip in his hand to boot. I don't know how he did it. Anyway, the only taxi in town at that time was old Josh, when he felt like it and wasn't likkered up. I didn't think I would bother to call him, so I said I would give the dwarf a ride if it wasn't too far because I had business to attend to. He said he wanted to drop by the Albright place and then go on up to the Nordquist house. So I took him.

Was Alice at home?

Yes, she was, and he treated her like the Queen of Sheba throwing a lot of flowery words her way about what a true companion she was to Paul and how even his descriptions hadn't done justice to her beauty. Made her a little queasy, I think, but Alice has always been nice if a little unusual.

What do you mean by unusual?

Well, she grew up without any proper folks, just an old aunt who didn't have much gumption. And the other children didn't seem to take to her, so she just sort of lived in her own world.

We hope she'll be safe traveling alone,

What's she going out west for?

She's looking for one of her sons.

She told you about her sons?

Yes. You seem surprised.

She brought em into the store when they were little tots. Kept apologizing because they ran up and down the aisles knocking things over.

How old were they when you saw them?

I never said I saw them. Now you got a good chance to make a crack, like did you often get invisible children in the store? No, I would say that Alice's were the only ones. You want my theory?

Yes,

I think they were practice children until the real ones came.

Did the real ones come?

No.

May we return to the Professor?

All right.

So from the Albright house you took the Professor to the House of Nordquist?

That's right. To tell the truth the idea of driving right up to the door of that place interested me. In the truck I said to the dwarf, say, you ain't in some kind of show up there, are you? How did you guess, he said, which took me back. Well, I said, you got the knack of speechifying.

What did he say to that?

He said he wished he could get me in to see the show, but it was a private performance. Said he was the evil troll under the bridge, where he cooked small children for supper. I don't like it too much when somebody gets smart-alecky with me, even a customer in the store, so I said you're dressed for the part all right. He said he might find me a part in the show, needed an Ichabod, could I ride a horse. I had to laugh at that. I could see I wasn't going to get the last word. I asked him what his connection to Paul was.

I'd be interested to know the answer he gave.

Said he was a friend for a long time. I told him I didn't know Paul had ever been in a carnival. He let that pass. Anyway, I said, Paul needs a friend of just about any kind. Why is that, he asked. Because, I said, he's up to the Nordquist place a lot and it ain't a regular place. What's the matter with it? One thing, it's all closed up, been like that for years. Paul's got a nice girl, Alice Coulter. He ought to marry her and go to a bigger town with more opportunities. But I don't think I'm telling you anything new.

Had you ever been in the house?

I'd say not. Nobody had. But we listened. Summer nights back when Paul was off to college they would crank open those big windows, ports they called them, and you could hear the old man hollering orders to the crew. Arctic storms in August. It was strange. But nobody wanted to say anything. It was the only interesting thing around here. It's been quiet since he died. I hear his boy is building something in the house.

How did you know the ship was sailing through an Arctic storm?

How? You could hear the old man shouting at the helmsman hard a-starboard, hard a-port, mind that floe, reef the mainsail and all like that. It was gripping. You got to pulling for the old man to make it through.

Through to where?

Don't know. Just on into the ice. Couldn't of been any ports that far north.

So what did you observe when you got to the house?

The first thing I observed was that the truck complained about going up that steep road, rough as a cob, but we made it to the door, only one in the house as far as I could see. The dwarf hopped out with his grip and wanted to know if I would accept a token of his gratitude. I said I would not since I could not see the show, pouty-like. It's a tragedy he said. Do you like tragedies? No, I said. There's enough of that in real life. And then he did a funny thing.

What was that?

He stopped several feet in front of the door and began to inch forward like he was afraid of stepping on one of those land mines buried everywhere anymore. I watched him until he finally inched up to the door and knocked and the woman in the robe let him in, the old man's widow. It must've taken him five minutes to get to the door. Nothing exploded. Maybe the explosion was inside that night. But I got another theory.

What's that?

That they put on the tragedy and something backfired. Say the dwarf was the villain creeping around with a big candle holder and he held it up to the drapes and caught the whole place on fire, all those crates piled up for years. The place was a tinderbox.

So it was truly a tragedy.

Yes. Paul was never the same. He went into himself, which meant that Alice had to go along with him if she wasn't going to leave him. That's all I know.

You have been very helpful, sir. We appreciate your time.

If you find out anything more, everybody would sure like to know it.

* * *

*My Beloved Nomad,*

*Sounds corny, doesn't it? I got it from an old movie. All you see on the screen is a lacy piece of stationery with a royal shield on it and the hand of the queen writing. Her fingers are all studded with diamonds and emeralds. This is her last letter to Lord Vallancourt because the scandal has caught up with them. My hand is a little different. I thought of getting some costume jewelry rings, but what would that signal to my fellow travelers? Right now my hands are getting stronger, carrying this grip through all these bus stations.*

*How many bus stations do you think there are in America? I've counted over 1,650 in the printed promo folder. That's just actual stations, not all the stops. It's the stops that kill you. You look out the window at the cactus and wonder if the bus is being held up by armed bandits from south of the border because you can't see even a shed. Nobody gets off or gets on. Maybe the bus driver has a girlfriend in a shack up off the highway, but you can't see it. Everybody that's been napping wakes up and tries to rub the fog off the window, which only smears the glass.*

*I didn't have to run away from anybody to make this trip. My husband Paul wrote down a number he got on the phone and then left the house. He's down in New York City chasing after an old friend while at the same time some government agents are chasing after him. It's all about the old fire. You remember, I told you about it. I don't think all this sleuthing will come to much. I told the agents I was planning a trip to see you. They thought I was really planning to go down to the City and look for Paul. Now they know better because they put a tail on me, if you can imagine. I spotted him in Paducah, Kentucky dressed like a hick. I feel sorry for him, traveling these roads he doesn't know where to, or what for. I thought of going up to him and speaking in a kindly way, but it would just be awkward for him and might even get him fired.*

*You are probably thinking that only an addled woman would write a letter that can't be mailed. Don't worry. I'll find you. It's in the cards. I didn't make it as a medium, but I have good intuitions. I'll know when I get close to you. It's like that old game we used to play when you were a kid. I'd hide something and then tell you you're getting warmer. Now you're getting colder, warmer, warmer. You're getting hot. It's like this trip, real zigzag but you get to see some of the wonders of this great country of ours.*

*The place where you are is getting painted in my mind. One time in my life I used to look at a lot of paintings. Anyway, your painting is what they call a mesa in the old westerns. You can't see anything on the horizon in any direction except air and sand. Which is very different from where I've been all my life til now looking up at a ridge and down at a river. Won't you be surprised when I walk up to you in some old saloon where your horse is tied up outside* to a post and hand you the letter and say, here's a letter from your mother.

I would have been happy to bring my husband Paul along. It would have done him good to get away out here in the west, but he's inside a bubble, which he carried with him down to in the City. It's been like that for twenty years. It's sad what a thing like a fire can do to a person. It didn't help that he had a friend you would have to call bad company who twisted his mind. So he's out of my life. And as for your brother, it's believed that maybe he got caught in the fire. So, until I can prove different, which I think I will someday, there's just you and me for now.

I'll be seeing you soon.

*With much love,*
*Your Mother*

* * *

*Director*
*National Division A*
*A.P.O. D Box 3489*

*Installment #6*

This will be my final report. It will be long because I have to write it in one sitting or memory will lose its focus. It will be taxing. I'll give you the best approximation I can of what Albright said during what I am sure was his last visit.

Here you have a mixture of voices—Albright's, the voice of a personage I will call the Guide, and the voices of other actors in the drama, as well as mine. So we have a case of double distortion—words filtered through Albright's heightened state of anticipation, and now through my imperfect memory. A formidable challenge, Director, to penetrate these layers and get back to the thing itself. But I am informed that in the world of intelligence you are a nonpareil.

*A little more groundwork. It's likely that until very recently Albright did not fully understand how deeply committed he was to the search he's now engaged in. His commitment lay dormant all those years since the fire. I suspect his wife knew this, at least intuitively, and disapproved, but had no way to discourage it.*

*Albright was a man of thought, not action, though a part of him longed to act. Now he is virtually the opposite, a creature with such a fierce will to act that it is dangerous to be near him, as your agents disastrously discovered. I deeply regret that I did not succeed in conveying that to them. How did Albright's powers—all unwilled and entirely without malice—come upon them? In my imagination their images would have been stripped from them before their selves disappeared. I'm afraid that sounds bizarre.*

*I'm not much given to moral philosophy, Director. From my school days to my business days to the corrections of my person in Manaus to the quiet shade of my garden my interest has always been in the mysteries of the self. Consequently, I don't ask myself whether I should have phoned Albright the number, or why I did. The number did not have his name attached. There it was on my doorstep on a four by six index card. My gardener picked it up as he returned from shopping and brought it to me where I was sitting under my little thatched gazebo, as I am now. The card was stippled with sunlight that pierced minutely the thatching of the roof. The number was long but otherwise unexceptional. I sensed immediately, however, that it had something to do with Paul Albright. I don't know why. I am not a numerologist. I called Albright and he came to the City, the City of Cain he'd been taught in college. Later, after much importuning on the part of your agent, I reluctantly gave him the number. I should have known it was dangerous. How? There were only common integers, no ominous symbols or Greek characters. Anyway, I was sure that your agents could not decipher the number, that it would lead nowhere and teach them that the search for Albright would be forever fruitless. I was wrong.*

*I return to Albright and the Guide, whom he met far to the south of my garden on a waterfront street in a district I have always avoided. It is an unnatural place built on debris euphemistically called fill. I do not know how the rendezvous was arranged. The eas-*

iest thing to say is that an unswerving seeker will sooner or later find a Guide who, detecting the seriousness of the seeker, will consent to take the seeker's hand so to speak.

Albright recognized the Guide immediately. He wore an un-fashionable suit, tight coat, snug vest with a watch fob on a gold chain looped from a large bone button to a small pocket nearby. These details, Director, Albright gave with a trace of fond remi-niscence, but that mode of rendering was short-lived. Presently he snapped his eyes back to me and fixed me with a curious look, as if he'd temporarily lost the sense of my presence. This gaze filled me with fear. I need not explain. I begged him go on with his story.

The Guide asked what he wanted. Albright said that he wanted to know the whereabouts of Eric Nordquist, who he believed might also know certain things he was interested in. Such as what, the Guide wanted to know. Such as the whereabouts of a certain book of paintings and how Helene was kept alive all those days on the stone and who started the fire at the House of Nordquist. The Guide asked Albright if he'd thought carefully about the consequences of possess-ing this knowledge. When Albright affirmed that he had, the Guide declared that he could guarantee nothing, but immediately led him down a steep declivity until they reached a muddy hollow. Above and around stood a dim line of buildings of irregular heights like the serrated mouth of an old hag. Albright-the-poet's metaphor.

The Guide said to Albright that they would be visiting the re-mains of three people lost in the fire that destroyed the House of Nordquist. One of them would not be his wife's younger son. Albright said that he already knew that. Good, said the Guide, because he does not exist, not even as an ectoplasm in one of your wife's séanc-es. Neither does the older son exist. The Guide's tone was pitiless, Albright said. It always had been. No student ever came to him for succor. They came to him as one might apply an astringent to an itch.

The two of them walked through sucking mud to an old house built on pilings driven down into tidal debris and muck.

I am no doubt diminishing, Director, the emotional charge of Albright's account for fear that its intensity would render these lurid details even more improbable.

*To go on. In all stories of this kind there is a menacing guard at the entryway. Albright spoke of prowling dogs and derelicts. The Guide scattered them with a fierce gaze and the pointing of a finger, as if aiming at them something far more destructive than a bullet. Albright paused and made a wry smile. You remember, he said, what it was like to be in that line of fire, God's laser.*

*Once inside the house they encountered a congeries of halls and stairs deeper and darker than the underground of the House of Nordquist. The Guide snapped on a broad beam flashlight and lit the way down a windowless passageway. Fetid air rose from decomposed wood and plaster. They arrived at a door sagging on its hinges. The Guide opened the door without knocking and entered the room peremptorily, beckoning Albright to come forward and stand beside him. The two of them looked down at a skeletal creature illuminated by the flashlight's beam. It lay supine on an indeterminate gray surface. A pair of atrociously bright eyes rolled toward the visitors, no eyelids, no canthi, only an edging of charred skin where a face was to have been.*

*This one, said the Guide, referring to the creature as one might a cadaver on a gurney, communicates only in incinerated bursts. Our inquiry will necessarily be cursory.*

*Albright, looking at the body of the creature, essentially an arrangement of barely articulated bones, wondered how she could make any noise at all. He turned to the Guide. Ask her how she was kept alive all those days on the stone.*

*That is not the question you came to ask, said the Guide harshly, but you have asked it. Answer, he commanded the creature. There came up from the heap of bones a low ruction attended by a barely audible metallic trilling. Albright saw that a nail had been driven through what looked like an x-ray simulation of a larynx. Then came words. Ich habe alles aufgegeben.*

*Auf Englische bitte! said the Guide as if scolding a refractory student.*

*I haf given up all.*

*That does not answer the question.*

*Ich kann nicht starben. Ich möchte lösen.*

*Auf Englische!*

*I cannot die. I want let go.*

*You had your chance to die, but you came back to the stone day after day.*

*They feed me.*

*What did they feed you?*

*Flesh.*

*What flesh?*

*Meine . . .*

*You ate your own flesh?*

*Nein. My flesh is in the music.*

*Whose flesh did you eat?*

*I cannot know.*

*You should have spat it out.*

*Ich möchte starben.*

The Guide turned to Albright. *You remember,* he said, *there are three deaths before resurrection—the death of the body, the death to sin, and the death of desire. Here we have a common paradox. She desires death and therefore cannot have it. She desired death in the ship, on the island, in the House of Nordquist. She is steeped in sin. It is not for us to desire death. Death is a gift.* He turned to the creature. *Who started the fire?*

*Das Feuer kam . . .*

*Auf Englishe!*

*The fire came everywhere. All the house went into it.* The voice cracked.

*She doesn't know. Here the residents are compelled to tell the truth except for those in the bottom rooms.* He turned to the creature. *Where is the black book of paintings?*

*I could never see.*

The Guide said to Paul, *we will get no more from her.* But the creature spoke again. *Aber wir haben die gros Idee.*

The Guide turned to Albright. *Yes, they had a grand idea. An assault on the Godhead. And you were there.*

*I was only a witness.*

*Be careful that you tell the truth. You might find yourself a resident here.*

*Kommen Sie hier nicht!*

*Danke, Frau. There. She has given you good advice. We will go now.*

*Director, I pause briefly to note, no doubt more for my own benefit than for yours, that we have here a sequence of transfer: flesh to Helene, Helene to the machine, the machine to the sounding sarcophagi. But the sequence is not complete at either end. Maybe no sequence ever is. I go on.*

*Out in the hall again the smell almost overcame Albright— fouled sea, rotting wood, decayed flesh. Albright's descriptive powers were so great that the stink of the place rose up around us, overcoming the fragrances of the garden. He got up from his chair and paced around the table. Maybe he wanted the illusion of walking away from that underground place. The name Alice was spoken. I apologize, Director, but I don't know why. Then bitterly the word twenty. Twenty years waiting for something to appear in the window, the annunciation that never came.*

*He sat back down and looked at me with an unbearable sharpness. Was I competent to hear the story or was I an obtuse dolt? How does one put on the look of competence? My face must have revealed my struggle to understand as surely as one of your polygraphs reveals deceit.*

*The Guide led Albright to another door, a bi-fold with pale light seeping through the slats. He grasped the knob of the door and pulled it open forcibly against a creaking resistance. What Albright saw at first was a surface welted with indistinct black. Hillocks of muted shine and lightless crevices revealed nothing beyond their own surfaces. Speak, commanded the Guide. Who are you?*

*A pair of twisted and blistered lips appeared, within them a ramshackle cage of blackened teeth and within that a tongue raked by fire. I was mother and painter of the great symphony*

*You forgot you were also procuress at hell's gate, said the Guide matter-of-factly. Where did you get the flesh you fed Helene?*

*Swaddlings.*

*Your own?*

*No.*

*Alicia's?*

*Babies are everywhere. In trains, in dreams.*

*Do dream babies have flesh?*

*Enough.*

*The Guide turned to Albright. Now you know how Helene was kept alive. He turned back to the charred creature. Did Helene know this?*

*Eric changed them into music.*

*Did he change your paintings into music?*

*No, it was the other way around.*

*Where is the book of paintings?*

*Eric has it.*

*Where is Eric?*

*I do not know.*

*Did he change the music into fire, or was it the fire into music?*

*He can change anything into music.*

*The Guide cocked his ear mockingly. We must bring him here to provide some musical entertainment for us.*

*No!*

*The Guide shut the door on the voice. He said to Albright, there is one more. Do you want to go deeper or have you seen enough of your old friends?*

*I want to go deeper.*

*Corruptio optimi pessima. You understand?*

*Yes, the corruption of the best is the worst.*

*I have to stop here, Director. I will keep my promise to write this final installment in one sitting, but I must lean back now and rest for a while.*

\* \* \*

Dear Son,

I got rid of the tail. It was easy. It's in all the old movies. You go into the ladies room and change your dress. You throw your grip out the window and climb out and catch a cab at the end of the alley. At the beauty parlor they make you into a strawberry blond with rosy *lipstick. Nothing that's an obvious disguise. You get big sunglasses that cover half your face. The hinges of the temple pieces are tiny little gold six-shooters. They're all the rage out here. I got a necklace made of turquoise beads, pure Navajo. I threw the old grip in a humpty-dumpster and got one made out of fake alligator skin. I got some designer jeans, but not too showy with iron studs or zippers. I don't look a day over thirty. You'll see.*

*I feel sorry for the tail. He might lose his job. I took a train out of town and sat by an old widower I knew was dying to talk because of the way he was tapping his fingertips together. Anybody looking around would think we were together. I pretended to be real interested in his family tree, three wives and lots of kids and grandkids. A very restless type. Didn't know what to do with himself now. I listened, but I didn't feel like I could help him at this point.*

*I've got to hand it to you. You're a great scenery picker. I never would've thought of coming to a place like this. Looking out the window I saw a great big rock perched on another pointy rock. It looked like a head suck on the end of a spear like in one of those old movies with cruel sultans. There were lots of rocks carved by the wind into waves and another rock that was stretched out between two pillars like the hypnotized lady they lay end to end across two chairs and the hypnotist stands on her stomach. I had doings with a lady lying on a stone once a long time ago. I'll tell you about it sometime.*

*You probably think I'm not going to recognize you because you never send photos of yourself, but the family resemblance will be too strong for me to miss. And who knows, you might recognize me. I can't wait to hear firsthand about some of those exciting places you've been. Maybe we can go to one together. My credit card is not down too low. If my husband Paul shows up, which he won't, you'll like him OK. He's the quiet type. I feel I'm getting closer to you now. Vibes they call it. It's something you'll get to know about me, the things I know without any numbers or facts.*

*OK, we're pulling into some big town. I don't know the name of it. I missed the sign, but I'm getting warm.*

*Your loving Mom Hot on the Trail.*

* * *

*(4 hours later. I napped, but did not sleep well. I am still tired and on edge, but I will complete my report at this sitting.)*

We will go deeper then, the Guide said. Follow me. The beam of his flashlight searched out the turns in the long corridor they walked.

At this point, Director, I looked up at the weatherless sky. I thought to myself I should have been the last of men to accompany another in an hallucinatory descent. But there I was in a hellhole of black night and stench. I looked at Albright. Why was he not overborne by the darkness of his tale? Maybe because he was inured to dark places: the bowels of the House of Nordquist, the nighttime windows of his kitchen, the shadowed passages of his own mind.

The two went down an uneven staircase, the risers and treads threatening collapse at every step. At the bottom they entered an indefinite darkness that Albright said had the feel of an empty vestibule. The Guide kept the beam of light on the cracked floor. Well, Sir Ghost, are you going to say something to us? Look whom I've brought you. Silence. The Guide turned to Albright. Note, the famous word monger declines to speak. Even to his beloved Childe Paul.

I would speak with him, said the Ghost, but a noxious presence constrains me.

If it weren't for what you call the noxious presence your visitor would not be here.

Ha. It was ever thus, was it not, Childe Paul? Our joyless interloper, master of quaint and dour theological interruptions. Yet endure him we must. He has certain prerogatives here.

In the silence that followed Albright heard a soughing as of many persons breathing laboriously, and a sliding as of many feet. Don't trouble yourself with the chorus, said the Ghost. They're an ignorant lot. When the fateful peripeteia comes, they always turn the wrong way and see only blood at the crossroads, which appeals to their love of spectacle.

The Guide said, our visitor wants to know who started the fire at the Nordquist house and why. Perhaps you can regale him with a tale of glorious self-immolation performed for the common good.

*I will come to the fire in good time. Did I ever tell you, Childe Paul, about the dinner I had with the Nordquists many years ago, long before I knew you?*

*No.*

*I remind you, said the Guide to Albright, that only here in the depths the truth is not required, though you might think it just the opposite. But let's listen. Everything is interesting that comes from the great man of words.*

*The Ghost ignored the Guide's disparagements. We dined in the wardroom. I knew the moment I entered that I had been there before, that I knew the Nordquists from old. Above an oblong expanse of a table covered with green felt hung the familiar ship's lantern burning with a smokeless flame, casting light through four panes—two clear, one green, one red. The lantern swayed with the gentle rolling of the ship. A shroud of gelid air hung by the bulkhead on the outboard side of the table and flowed across the deck and under our feet. The old man sat at the head of the table, Deirdre on one side, the boy on the other, and I at the other end. Behind Deirdre in the penumbra of the lantern's glow was another presence. Later, on signal from Deirdre, the presence would produce a series of broken tones that beat for a moment against the inboard bulkhead and then hung pinioned there like a withered espalier. We had crystal goblets of a strong amber drink. The old man was quickly drunk. Nord! Nord! he shouted more and more frequently. Where? asked the red-haired boy of the red-haired father. Null! Null! shouted the old man.*

*The boy laughed. I never heard such laughter from man or boy. Utterly without emotion, forged in white heat like tempered steel.*

*An apt figure, said the Guide, for an arsonist.*

*The Ghost did not deign to make reply. Many years later, he said, when I came to the House of Nordquist again, though you warned me not to, Deirdre sought to put between me and my intention many clever deviations. She took me on an excursion along the brow of the hill. It was a lovely late afternoon. The fibers of her gray caftan were joyously aroused by the slant glow of the golden sun. A flock of small birds came sweeping over the hillside all aflutter, their piping so gay and infectious that Deirdre and I laughed together. A moment later she directed my attention to a bright bushy thing just rising up over* the crest of the hill. A girl child with wild hair now appeared skipping across the dry grasses, stopping just before she reached Deirdre. Who was I and why had I come, she asked in a tone almost impertinent. I was a Professor, Deirdre said. Had I come to teach Eric words and numbers? I told her I had not. Good, because others have tried, she said saucily and scampered away. We went back to the house. Deirdre left me at the door, hatchway I should say, of my room. I stood wondering what I had been shown.

I'm surprised you bothered to wonder, the Guide said. You had already conflated past and future and determined that the lady's gray wool would be converted into white ash.

The Ghost laughed dryly. O Reverend Theologian, try to shuck your literalism just for a while. To proceed, Childe Paul, with Deirdre's deviations. The room in which the saintly mother put me housed many contrivances more hackneyed than cunning. A funhouse mirror, warbled and silvered with dazzling undercoating, so painful to look into that tears stained my spectacles if I even glanced into it. Trompe l'oeil walls painted to look like steel bulkheads. Desk and chairs bolted to the deck in case of foul weather. A bunk with high sides and straps so that the sleeper would not be pitched out onto the deck during storms. And distant music, of course, sometimes swift and soaring, sometimes mournfully plangent.

The Guide sighed loudly. Our guest has come seeking answers to certain questions, about the firebrand and his motives. I don't have time for these inventions. I have other visitors waiting for me.

This is not a confessional, the Ghost said. If my motives are not by now perfectly clear, then you are an even worse hermeneut than I thought.

All this time, Director, Albright had stood silent beside the Guide, listening. Now he said, someone got away.

No one got away. And now it is time, Childe Paul, for you to go home. This is no place for you.

The one who got away took the book with him, Albright said.

No book was saved by anyone, much less by the son of a delusional mind. I do not mean to be cruel. Go home, Childe Paul.

The Guide said, if you are waiting for an affectionate parting, you are wasting your time. There is no love here.

The Ghost spoke again, overcoming reluctance. *You and I were for a while deluded. Blowing our horn at the entrance to a dark tower. Open to us the gate of deliverance, O great Weltumformer, abjurer of words, conqueror of self, you who have sailed to the edge of absolute zero and come back. Establish the Novum Ordo Seclorum, O ruler of stone and fire, alchemist of music and flesh. We thought we had arrived at the cosmic crux. We were deluded. But now he is done, the danger past. Go home, Childe Paul.*

Now a chorus of moans, feet shuffling, fading away.

*Well and truly spoken for once, Nemo. And so you appointed yourself to perform the purification by fire like some old Hindu.*

Albright, looking into the glassy eyes of the Ghost, saw the hint of a tear.

The Ghost spoke more urgently. *What if you found him? Do you intend to bring him before the law? The law killeth. The spirit giveth life. Even your doleful docent could tell you that. Have you told him, Theologian, why you are consigned to be a guide in the Underworld?*

The Guide spoke in a voice less edged. *I too was once deluded. I thought in those early days at Justin and James when Nemo and I contended for possession of the Logos that I was fighting the Anti-Christ, that under that little black beret and in that twisted body resided the Zeitgeist of this poisonous age. Avatars of Socrates and Protagoras, we were, in heroic combat. I was deluded. It is for hubris I am condemned for a certain season to escort visitors to this dreadful house. The Professor gave you good advice. You have your answers. Who fed another forbidden flesh. Who ignited the fire and why. About these things he chose to speak the truth. Now go home.*

*Where is the book, Albright asked.*

*Lost, burned, shredded by the acids of age. It matters not.*

The two left the Ghost, who offered no valediction. They climbed the stairs and opened the door of the house. Albright stepped out onto the unevenly cobbled street. The crepuscular glow of the city, he said, was as abhorrent as the darkness of the house.

Back in the gazebo Albright got up from his chair. I hoped he would tell me that he was going home. But he stood looking down at the empty chair. And then to my amazement he began to smile. Do you remember, he said, the desk and its deskness?

*Yes, I said.*

*Do you remember the Meachem who had no origin?*

*Yes, I said. Is this a catechism of memories?*

*Do you remember the log that brought down the pile?*

*Yes.*

*How did you know which one it was?*

*I saw that it was the right one, I said.*

*How?*

*I don't know.*

*I'll tell you how. All the other logs disappeared from your field of vision. Isn't that right?*

*I know where you're going with this. It won't work.*

*Why?*

*Because the German put together a microcosm of wood. I could walk all the way around it. I could see all its parts. I could bracket out the stable pieces. But you, you have the whole world to walk around, and it will be changing every minute you walk it.*

*You're thinking of the poem we studied about world enough and time.*

*I don't remember the poem. If it said there is world enough and time for anything at all it was wrong. You're not going to find Eric. You would have to stop and look at hundreds of millions of houses. Some of them would burn down before you got to them and you would have to rummage among the ashes. How long will you have to stand looking at each house before you can bracket it out? And all that time you will be a menace to anybody who comes near you. Give it up. Go back to Alice.*

He said nothing to that, Director. He gave me a pitying look, as if I had understood nothing after all. Actually I did understand. He conceived of his life as a choice between hundreds of millions of houses and nothingness. Well, he is gone now. It is not for me, Director, to give advice to one in your station, but you know what I would say. You will pursue him at great risk. If you get between a person intent on finding the absolute and something he believes might house the absolute, you confront a lethal intention. It's not a place. If it were a place, it would have coordinates. Your agents could get the right numbers. One time, early in my transactions with Albright and your *agents, I thought I might construct a speculum designed especially for this case. With it one would be able to distinguish realities from phantasmagoria. How foolish. So I have nothing for you but the tale itself.*

*I end by saying that I have endeavored to be truthful in even the smallest detail. Memory is flawed. Perception is fractional and even that bit of seeing is refracted as in a warbled mirror. For all that, I truly hope that I have been useful to you.*

*Sincerely,*
*Thomas Meachem*

* * *

*Dear Son,*

*I don't need to tell you how thrilled I was to get your letter and an address for you at last. And it came just at the right time. I'm here with your brother. I found him in a lean-to upside a big rock face. He was talking to an Indian and cooking a rattlesnake. Can you believe it?*

*Please come out and be with us at least for a little while. I'm not going to try to make him settle down, but I'm not going to let him get away again either. We bought a Camaro convertible, silver. It's old, 1969, but that's OK. Nothing rusts out here in the desert. I don't know if the top is really waterproof or not, but it never rains. No doubt we'll be going from place to place because that's his nature, but I will keep sending you addresses until you arrive. I can hardly wait. It's been so long.*

*He's glad you're coming too though he's not a real people person. The strong silent type. Spent too long in places where he was a stranger or like here looking at the distant horizon. But I'll bring him around. I learned some things trying to bring my husband around even if I didn't always succeed. We'll see.*

*It will be great the three of us together. Like they say in the old movies, it will be the crown of my life.*

*Your loving mother,*
*Alice*

## ABOUT THE AUTHOR

Eugene K. Garber has published five books of fiction and is the creator, with eight other artists, of *EROICA*, a hypermedia fiction (http://hypereroica.com/). His fiction has won the Associated Writing Programs Short Fiction Award and the William Goyen Prize for Fiction sponsored by *TriQuarterly*. His awards include fellowships from the National Endowment for the Arts, the National Endowment for the Humanities, and the New York State Council of the Arts. His short fiction has been anthologized in *The Norton Anthology of Contemporary Fiction* (1988), *Revelation and Other Fiction from the Sewanee Review*, *The Paris Review Anthology*, and *Best American Short Stories*.

CPSIA information can be obtained
at www.ICGtesting.com
Printed in the USA
BVOW08s0443020418
512146BV00001B/1/P